Praise for Jess Dee's *Ask Adam*

5 Angels—and a Recommended Read. "It is one of the hottest books that I've ever read...The sexual tension between Adam and Lexi is so thick from the second that they make their first connection that you can feel it. ... Great job Ms. Dee, I'll be looking for more of your books!"

~ *Missy, Fallen Angel Reviews*

5 Stars "Wow! Jess Dee has certainly written a winner with Ask Adam...Anyone who enjoys well written characters, lots of scorching hot sex and solid story will enjoy Ask Adam. I know I did!"

~ *Trang, Ecataromance*

5 Red Roses "This is a powerful, sensual love story. The sex scenes explode off the page, but there is much more than just sex to this riveting tale. Written with style and flair, this book grabs you from the start and holds you to the end. Highly recommended!"

~ *Anne, Red Roses for Authors*

5 Cupid's for plot and romance "Ask Adam is a fantastic read... The dialogue and writing style were excellent and kept the reading fresh and exciting."

~ *Marina, Cupid's Library Reviews*

Look for these titles by
Jess Dee

Now Available:

Photo Opportunity

Coming Soon:

Circle of Three Series
Only Tyler

Ask Adam

Jess Dee

A Samhain Publishing, Ltd. publication.

Samhain Publishing, Ltd.
577 Mulberry Street, Suite 1520
Macon, GA 31201
www.samhainpublishing.com

Editing by Carrie Jackson
Cover by Scott Carpenter

First Samhain Publishing, Ltd. electronic publication: September 2007
First Samhain Publishing, Ltd. print publication: July 2008

Dedication

With special thanks:

To Bev, Frances and Bernie, for their unfailing support, advice, wisdom and encouragement.

To Carrie Jackson, for her tireless and ingenious efforts to make this book the best it could be.

And, as always, to my boys—I love you!

Chapter One

Lexi Tanner made her way resolutely through the lobby. The only thing standing between her and fifty thousand dollars was a polite-looking receptionist.

She flashed the man her most dazzling smile. "Hello there. I'm looking for a guest here at the hotel. Could you tell me what room Mr. AJ Riley is in?"

The young man flashed a dazzling smile straight back. "I'm sorry, ma'am. I'm not at liberty to give you that information."

Bugger. She'd figured that would probably happen but she'd had to give it a try anyway. "Perhaps you could ring his room and let him know he has a visitor?"

"To be honest, ma'am, I'm not sure he's there. I saw him leave a couple of hours ago."

"Well, I guess it's still worth a try." She had to see Riley today. She was too excited not to.

The man lifted a receiver and dialed. Surreptitiously, Lexi tried to see which buttons he'd pushed, but the counter hid the phone.

He covered the mouthpiece with his hand. "And whom may I say is calling?"

Lexi floundered for a second. She didn't particularly want a hotel clerk introducing her over the phone. "I'm a representative from the conference. I want to thank him for his generous sponsorship."

He shook his head. "Mr. Riley's not answering. Would you like to leave a message?"

Biting her lip, Lexi considered this possibility. Unless Riley's secretary had given him a rundown of all his upcoming appointments, he wouldn't have a clue who she was. She didn't feel like explaining it on an answering machine, or worse, in a memo scrawled on hotel notepaper. Nope. She'd prefer to introduce herself in person.

"No, thank you. I'll try again later."

The newspaper article had specified that Riley was staying at the same hotel. How could fate be so cruel? Putting her so close to him and then preventing them from meeting. It just seemed mean. She walked away, trying not to feel too peeved. If all else failed, she still had her official appointment with him in Sydney next week. But since they were both in Melbourne now, she'd do what she could to meet him before then. Tea break wasn't too far off. Perhaps he'd be back by then.

A thought occurred to her. If Riley'd left his hotel room, perhaps he was downstairs, in this very lobby, right now. Who knew? She scanned the grand entrance of the hotel. It didn't matter that she'd never met him before and had no idea what he looked like. She knew she'd recognize him the minute she laid eyes on him. Over the last six weeks of trying to track him down, she'd conjured up a pretty good mental image of him.

He had to be in his late fifties, early sixties. His multi-million dollar business meant he'd been around a while and built up his empire over a good few years. So she'd assigned him grey hair. Maybe silverish—a dash of elegance to fit the successful businessman image. He wore glasses—but only for reading—and had a kind smile. Anyone who donated the kind of money to charity that he did had to have a kind smile. For some inexplicable reason, she just knew he had a moustache. His clothes of choice were expensive suits, silk ties and polished shoes. Finally, she pictured him as slightly overweight. All those business lunches had to have taken their toll.

The quick once-over failed to reveal the man. Unfortunately, it also failed to reveal the small suitcase on the floor in front of her. Her ankle connected with the bag and solid ground slipped away from beneath her feet.

In the brief time it took to fly unceremoniously across the reception area of the five star hotel, Lexi realized in complete mortification that she would land spread-eagle on the floor in front of fifty or so complete strangers.

As the chandelier above her spiraled out of sight and the carpet loomed ever closer, something clamped around her upper arms with the power of iron manacles, effectively halting her downward plummet. While her body came to a screeching stop, her head kept moving, propelled forward by the force of her fall, until it slammed into something hard. A wall of hot, male muscle.

Struggling to catch her breath, Lexi grabbed hold of the first thing she could to steady herself. Her fingers closed around soft handfuls of expensive cotton, and the heat from beneath the material seared through her. The wall of muscle pulsated beneath her hands.

"Steady," a voice sounded in her ear, low and deep. Despite the precarious situation she found herself in, it sent shivers whistling down her spine. "I've got you."

The iron manacles eased their pressure but did not release her. Lexi shifted back a little so she could look into the face of the man who'd broken her fall.

As her eyes locked with his, her heart simply ceased

beating. Never before had attraction been so sudden or so fierce. His gaze trapped hers. His eyes weren't just cold—they were icy. They reminded her of a glacier glinting blue streaks beneath a winter sun. As she stared, aware of her heart beating once again, slowly at first, then faster and faster until it raced, she wondered how such cold eyes could fire up her body with just a look.

"You okay?" Again his voice unsettled her. It made the back of her neck tingle.

Winded and unable to speak, she nodded. It had nothing to do with her fall. His presence left her panting, searching uselessly for oxygen. His aftershave wafted around her, compounding her problem. Every time she managed to inhale, she caught his scent—spicy, earthy and dangerous and tinged with a splash of power. The man smelt of success.

She nodded again and cleared her throat. "I...uh...I'm okay."

Good grief, he was gorgeous. Drop-dead, heart-stopping, breathtaking gorgeous. Not to mention intriguing. Thick black hair framed his tanned skin and highlighted his straight nose, which screamed of affluence and arrogance. His chiseled and beautiful face had high cheekbones and a generous mouth. His lips stole her attention, though. They were set in lines so hard she wondered if he'd forgotten how to smile. He wore his features in a rigid mask and they showed no signs of softening.

She let go of his shirt. "Thank you. For catching me."

He said nothing, merely nodded and released her from his grasp, allowing a little distance between them. He stood a few feet away yet towered above her. A charcoal suit jacket hugged his broad, square shoulders. Lord, they weren't just broad; they hid the entire lounge behind him.

Wrinkles marked his shirt at the two points where she'd

clasped it in a death grip. Without thinking, she stepped forward and smoothed the creases. Beneath her ministrations, his stomach jerked, then tightened. She responded viscerally. Deep between her legs, she sprang to life in a gush of liquid heat.

She dropped her hands and stepped back. "I'm...sorry. Your shirt...I just..." She just what? Wanted to show her gratitude? Tried to cop a feel? Blushed a little? Got seriously turned on? All of the above? Besides, why apologize? She'd only tried to straighten his shirt. He'd gone and...and...well, flexed his stomach muscles. Jerked under her touch.

God help her, he stared at her now with undisguised hunger in those icy eyes. Looked at her as if she were breakfast. His lips parted and a hint of color tinged his cheeks. Sheer animal magnetism radiated off him. Desire shimmied through her unchecked, causing her breasts to swell.

He noticed. His gaze settled on her nipples, turning them into tight beads. His own chest expanded as he breathed deeply and then exhaled with a sharp hiss. The sound reverberated through her body, finely tuning those parts of her that were not already humming with need.

From behind, someone clapped him on the back, oblivious to the encounter unfolding between them. "Mate," said the newcomer, not noticing Lexi, "he's ready to talk figures."

Though he inclined his head to listen, the glacial eyes remained fixed on her. He nodded briefly in response and added a short, "Fine, let's do it."

That voice. It reverberated through her. An image of him whispering the same words to her swam before her eyes, an image of him leaning down, a hand tangling in her hair, his voice a suggestive breath in her ear. "Let's do it."

Oh. God, yes. Let's.

Only when she noticed the sensual gleam shimmering through the icy stare did she realize she'd whispered the words out loud. He'd had no trouble understanding their meaning.

"Perhaps another time," he answered, his voice a low growl.

She wanted to say something but could not think of a single appropriate answer. She couldn't think at all with those eyes feeding on her. Before she had a chance to speak, something resembling surprise flickered over his face. He blinked and straightened, snapping whatever invisible connection had cocooned them together.

Just like that, the moment passed.

"I'll get the car and meet you outside," his friend told him. "See you in five." He walked away.

The man gave her a sharp nod. "Please excuse me. I must go."

"Uh, yes, of course." Lexi shook her head to clear it. "Thank you again. For breaking my fall." She gave a stilted smile and forced herself to put one leg in front of the other while her heart hammered unevenly in her chest. "It was nice to meet you."

She walked toward the auditorium. The prickling sensation down her back told her the ice blue eyes followed her progress past the lounge and through the doors leading to the hall. Not once did she allow herself the pleasure, or humiliation, of looking back.

AJ Riley glanced at the sheet he'd been handed as he climbed into the car. He was barely able to focus on the bold print. The fine print streamed off the page in a jumble of letters.

"Are you sure about this?" his oldest friend and partner, Matt Brodie, asked.

The only thing AJ was sure about was the throbbing in his cock. Erect and stiff, it jutted out like a tent pole, ready for action. Unfortunately, he'd left the action and her hot, sexy body in the hotel lobby. Which left him aroused and out of luck.

Good thing he'd done up his jacket.

"Yeah, I'm sure." He forced his attention back to Matt. "The kid's built up a damn good company. Problem is, he's gone as far as he can and he knows it. We can turn the business around. If he agrees to stay on as managing director as opposed to outright owner, he'll make himself a lot of money. Fast."

Matt nodded. "Agreed." He motioned to the pages in AJ's hands. "If we apply a little pressure, we can have the numbers sorted by close of business today."

"Let's do it," AJ reinforced, and his partner replied. He didn't hear him. His concentration was shot.

Oh. God, yes. Let's.

She might as well have been standing butt naked in the hotel foyer, beckoning to him. That's how provocative her words had been. He was pretty sure she hadn't meant to say them out loud. The look of horror on her face bore testament to the fact. In truth, her words hadn't made a damn's worth of difference. Her thoughts had been scrawled across her face and her body, the heaving breasts and hard nipples a dead giveaway. She'd been just as turned on as he. Just as aware of the immediate connection.

He'd reacted the same way the last time he'd seen Lexi Tanner. His body had jolted to life the instant he'd laid eyes on her. Dammit, he hadn't liked the feeling then either. This time though, her presence hadn't just jolted him, it had almost electrocuted him. Like a thousand-volt jumpstart to his groin.

What about the look on her face? He was aware that she didn't know him, yet the instant she'd seen him, something had flashed in her eyes. Had it been recognition?

Shit, he hadn't meant to catch her, hadn't even realized she was in the hotel. He'd seen someone trip and couldn't just let her fall. Instinct had taken over and he'd thrown out his arms. How could he know that once he'd grabbed hold of her he'd find it almost impossible to let go?

Once before he'd held someone, determined never to let go. That time, he hadn't had a say in the outcome. This time he had. He'd released her.

CR

The conference—The National Congress on the Psychosocial Affects of Childhood Leukemias and Cancers—had yet to convene for the day, and people milled around outside the auditorium, sipping tea or coffee. Lexi approached them, more than a little shaken. The entire encounter with the man had lasted less then two minutes yet left an indelible impression. Attraction had never flared so fast. Her body still fluttered in anticipation of what he might have done to her. "Let's do it," he'd said and she'd responded. In reality, he'd addressed someone else.

Arousal washed over her, leaving her wet and horny and a little stunned. Sex wasn't something she took lightly. Uh uh. Not Lexi. She'd never sleep with someone on a whim. She had to know the man first, know him well before he got to see her naked. Yet, this guy... Hot damn, given half a chance, she'd drag him—kicking and screaming if need be—back to her room and have her way with him. Boy, oh boy, she wouldn't just have her way with him, she'd make love to him like there was no tomorrow.

For God's sake, try to look professional. You're about to walk into a room full of work associates. Think about Riley, get your focus back. Riley had simply slipped from her mind, like everything else, the second those hands clasped her arms. She was a goner. Lost in the feverish haze of desire.

"So, did you find him?" a voice asked over her shoulder. She answered yes instinctively, her mind occupied by flashes of those eyes.

"You saw AJ Riley?" Her friend and colleague, Leona Ramsey, gasped, walking around to stand next to her. "Did you speak to him?"

"Yes." Lexi shook her head. "I mean no." Leona knew she'd been tracking down Riley. "The hotel wouldn't even give me his room number."

Her friend gave her a strange look. "So you didn't meet him?"

"Didn't even come close." Lexi frowned and gave Leona a run down of her conversation with the receptionist.

Leona clicked her tongue. "Well that's just too bad, isn't it? What do you plan to do now?"

"Try again at tea. Maybe he'll be back at the hotel by then."

Leona narrowed her eyes. "Are you okay? You look kind of flushed."

"I'm fine," Lexi answered. *I've just fallen in complete lust and can't think of anything other than a night of sinful, sweaty sex. Other than that, I'm fine.*

"You sure?"

"Positive." *Although I'd be a lot better after three or four orgasms.*

"You're shaking," Leona pointed out.

Yeah, that's what happens when I get turned on. "Just hungry. I didn't eat very much at breakfast."

Leona lifted a platter of scones with jam from one of the tables and offered it to Lexi. "Looks like you could do with one."

"I could." Lexi took the food gratefully and bit into it. It was sweet and buttery and dry, not at all like the salty male flesh she really wanted to sink her teeth into.

Determined to carry on a normal conversation, she asked, "You all prepared for the talk?" Leona was about to address the hundred-odd audience in the auditorium about the latest developments in the treatments of childhood cancers and leukemias. Lexi managed to keep her attention focused on her friend's answer for at least thirty seconds before her stomach lurched and, unbidden, she heard him whisper in her ear, "Let's do it."

Chapter Two

The tea break found Lexi back at the front desk, asking the same receptionist to dial AJ Riley's room. He gave her a quizzical look. "You haven't seen him yet?" he asked.

"No..." Lexi replied, thinking the obvious—if she had, she wouldn't be here right now.

"Oh, I thought...never mind." He smiled at her as though to hide his confusion. "I can try his room. He returned earlier, but I believe he left again." After a couple of moments, he shook his head. "There's no response. Would you like to leave a message this time?"

Lexi shook her head. "No." She sighed. "I don't suppose he told you what time he'd be back?"

The receptionist answered with a deadpan face. "Most of our guests don't leave that kind of information with us."

Of course they didn't. It was worth asking—just in case. "Thank you. I'll try again later." She left as frustrated as before.

This time she managed to walk through the lobby without making a complete debacle of herself. Although she subtly scanned the area twice, there was no sign of either Riley or the complete stranger she'd so delicately bumped into earlier. She chose to ignore the pangs of disappointment that fluttered through her stomach.

The next three attempts at contacting Riley proved just as successful as the first two. Later, Lexi sat at dinner with Leona, feeling disheartened and disillusioned. The sooner she could meet Riley, the sooner she could convince him to donate the fifty thousand and the sooner she could start up the project.

It was a good program. She'd spent months drawing up the plans, which had approval from both the hospital board and the ward staff. A couple of nurses had even signed up to help. Now she needed the funding to get it off the ground—and she'd yet to make contact with the most probable source of that funding.

All her efforts today had come to nothing. Well, nothing except tripping in the lobby and landing with her nose mashed into the spectacular chest of "Superhunk".

Not a bad result, all things considered.

"Yoo-hoo. Hello? Earth to Lexi?" Leona waved her hand in front of Lexi's eyes.

Lexi blinked and grinned. "Sorry, I zoned out on you for a minute there."

"Yeah, I noticed."

"I guess I'm obsessing a little." She looked sheepishly at Leona. "I've just got to find Riley, Lee. He's right here, so close I can almost touch him."

"Don't you ever get tired of trying to raise money for POWS?" Leona asked, referring to the Pediatric Oncology and Hematology Ward at Sydney's Eastern Suburbs Hospital, where she worked as a pediatrician and Lexi worked as a social worker. "It's not even part of your job description."

"So tired I can hardly limp out of bed some mornings," Lexi answered. "It's just something I need to do. It's like I can't rest until I've done my bit to help."

"Retribution?"

Lexi shrugged. "In a sense, I suppose. I've been there, I know what it's like. Now I can use that knowledge to make the journey a little less tough for someone else."

"Your sister found it tougher," Leona pointed out. "She had leukemia."

"That is such a doctor comment to make. You only see the patient's point of view," Lexi griped good-naturedly, knowing Leona was teasing her. "Never mind the siblings and the rest of the family who go through the trauma of cancer."

Leona grinned. "Yeah, doctors. Go figure. Why would we want to focus all our attention on a sick child when there's a whole family out there who needs some loving care?"

Lexi smiled back. Leona always included the whole family in her treatment plan. As a general rule, doctors weren't trained to look after the emotional needs of the patient's family. As a social worker, Lexi was—but she knew she hadn't done a good enough job. Not yet. When she finished raising money for the sibling program, when she could provide better support for the brothers and sisters of children with cancer, then she'd put a little less pressure on herself.

"Lex," Leona said, her tone more serious. "I think you're moving too fast on this one. You've got too much riding on the program to screw it up. Wait for Wednesday to see Riley. Meet him when you're more prepared, when you have all your files and information with you."

"You're right, Lee. I know you are." Lexi squirmed in her seat. "It's just that he's here, in the same hotel... I can't wait. I have to see him."

"I think you're being impulsive," her friend warned. "You know how you tend to say the wrong thing when emotion takes over. Your mouth just runs off without you."

Darn. She did tend to shoot off her mouth when she got

excited, and meeting Riley was definitely something worth getting excited about. He was, after all, the person voted most likely to sponsor her program. So the chances were high she could say something she'd regret. But, c'mon. How could she not seize the moment? How could she let the opportunity of a lifetime blow right past her?

"I've got to do it, Lee. I've got to make the most of this time. Destiny's given me this chance. I'm going to jump at it. Of course I'll go to the appointment as well. I'd never cancel that." Excitement churned in her belly. "Look, I promise I'll check every word that comes out of my mouth. I will be the paragon of tact and diplomacy, but mark my words. On Wednesday, when I walk into his office, it will not be the first time I meet Mr. Riley. *That* I promise you."

CR

AJ's day had been a bitch. What started out as a friendly merger had almost turned into a hostile takeover. So much for talking numbers. The owner of the small company Riley Corporation planned to purchase had suddenly gotten cold feet and flat-out refused their more than generous offer.

Damn fool didn't have the sense to realize Riley Corporation was the best thing that could have happened to him. In six months, AJ expected to see a one hundred percent growth in profit, then double that in double the time. Good thing Matt had been there to talk a bit of sense into the bloke, because his own input today had been somewhat less than impressive. He could barely string an intelligible sentence together, let alone argue with the dumbass kid.

He'd been all screwed up since he'd caught her in the lobby this morning. Christ, the effect Lexi Tanner had on him. Only a miracle had prevented him from jumping her right there at the reception desk.

Four months earlier, he'd had a similar reaction to her. He'd attended a fundraising exhibition for POWS, organized by Lexi. Her brother, Daniel Tanner, had been the featured photographer. The minute AJ walked into the gallery he'd noticed her. She was hard to miss. She'd pulled his attention toward her with gravitational force, and for the next hour he'd been aware of her every movement.

During the process of purchasing several of Tanner's outstanding photographs—a charitable obligation to which he felt committed—he'd gathered as much information as he could about the social worker. Then he'd left, knowing one thing: Lexi symbolized big trouble. She embodied everything he had to stay far away from.

Unless, of course, he was willing to send himself to hell and back—for a second time.

AJ beeped the remote alarm of the rental car and caught the hotel lift up from the parking garage, almost tasting the double scotch waiting for him in his room. Fate had different ideas. The lift stopped at the ground floor and several people climbed in—including Lexi Tanner and her friend, Dr. someone or other. For the second time that day his body heated to a dangerous level.

Christ, she was gorgeous. Her hair tumbled down her back in a shower of golden curls. Full lips, a slightly tilted nose and thick black lashes made up a beautiful face. She probably reached around five-eight in heels and had curves in all the right places. Real, womanly curves.

He stared, unable to look away.

As she caught sight of him, she froze. The air between them sizzled and ignited. She consumed his senses. She stood close, so close he caught the scent of her perfume again. It was spicy and sexy and he'd smelled it the whole day. Some of it must have rubbed off on his jacket earlier when she'd tumbled into his arms.

Words were spoken. He didn't hear them. All his senses focused on her. Lexi apparently experienced the same phenomenon. Only when the doctor nudged her and said aloud, "Nineteen, please, and I'm on five," did he realized someone had asked her floor number.

A startled-looking Lexi turned to the man in question. She flashed him a smile. "I'm sorry. Nineteen, please."

If she smiled at him like that, even once, he'd have her backed up against the wall, her hands pinned at her sides and her chest squashed into his, before she had a chance to take another breath.

"What is with you today?" the doctor asked her. "That is about the fourth time you've zoned out on me."

Lexi turned back to AJ. The temperature climbed five degrees. He reached for his tie, loosening the knot at the base of his throat. Surely it would help him breathe? Her very presence penetrated deep in his body.

"Sorry, I'm a little sidetracked," she answered, still staring at him.

A bell rung. "That's my floor," her friend said. "Look, I'll see you at breakfast. Good luck, I hope you find him."

Find him? Who the fuck was she looking for? Last he'd heard, she wasn't involved with anyone. Ah, shit. Jealousy didn't sit well with him. He didn't want to show interest in Lexi. So why did the thought of her looking for another man have sparks of rage exploding in his gut?

Her gaze settled on his face. "Hello." She kept her voice low; aimed it at him and nobody else.

He nodded, shifted so someone behind him could get out of the lift, but did not look away.

She smiled. "I hoped I'd bump into you again."

He lifted an eyebrow, unable to speak—such was the effect of her presence on him.

"I wanted to thank you."

The lift dinged, signaling his floor. He stood motionless. How could he move? Her eyes pinned him down. They were an unexpected stormy grey. This morning they'd been a deep sapphire blue.

"You saved me from embarrassing myself earlier. I'm blushing just thinking about it." Yeah, her cheeks were flushed. Only she didn't look embarrassed. Her eyes were hooded, her pupils dilated and the smoky irises oozed desire. Framed by the color in her cheeks and the natural pout of her lips, she looked positively wanton.

Around them the lift emptied slowly.

"No problem." Christ, he shouldn't talk to her. He needed to get his ass the hell out of there.

She caught her lower lip between her teeth and nibbled, accentuating a sexy dimple on her left cheek. The action caught him in his stomach and left him reeling. He shifted again. His body stirred and blood thrummed in his ears.

Slowly releasing her lip, she said, "Dumb thing to do, tripping like that." She smiled. Not a friendly, grateful grin. No. This was a sensuous, knowing smile. A smile that told him she'd sussed him out, she knew his thoughts—and she found herself equally affected.

AJ was thirty-six years old, yet the look on her face reduced him to a kid. Need slammed into him and he knew against his better judgment that he had to have her.

He shrugged. "Accidents happen."

The lift dinged. The doors slid open and closed again. Then there were two of them. Two adults and the audible hum of awareness buzzing between them.

With no rationale to his thoughts, no premeditation to his movements, he did what he had to do. Stepping forward, he pushed a button. The lift ground to a halt somewhere between the seventeenth and eighteenth floors.

Her briefcase slid from her hand, landing on the floor with a soft thud.

"That the only reason you were hoping to bump into me?" he asked. "To thank me?"

"It was one of the reasons."

"There were others?"

She nodded. "Just one other." She raised her hand to his chest. Her slim fingers played provocatively with the buttons on his shirt.

"What...?" His question trailed off as she lowered her hand to his waist and stroked his stomach. Beneath her touch, his muscles contracted involuntarily.

"That's what." Her voice slid like velvet over his skin. "Before, in the lobby, when I touched you, you had the same reaction."

"You took me by surprise. I didn't expect you to touch me."

"I didn't expect you to respond."

Christ, what had she expected? That she'd brush her hands down his shirt and he'd whistle a merry tune? "Did you expect me to respond this time?"

"I hoped," she whispered as she toyed with his belt.

"I'm responding." His voice sounded hoarser than he would have liked but with the entire life force in his body concentrated on his dick, it was damn near impossible to hold a rational conversation.

"I can see."

Of course she could. He had a massive hard-on. If they'd taken separate lifts, she'd be able to see it. A bead of sweat formed on his back and trickled down between his shoulder blades. He shuddered with the need to touch her. She noticed and smiled again. The sinuous, womanly smile that played havoc with his self-control.

Damn it. AJ was the master of control. Control meant predictability and his life needed to be predictable. No more nasty surprises—ever. He'd learned the hard way some things could not be easily manipulated—but that which he could influence, he did. Women were no exception to the rule.

So why did the ripple of her very delectable breasts make his logic take flight?

"If it helps, I'm responding too." Her chest rose and fell unsteadily, pulling his attention downwards.

A button had popped open near the top of her tailored navy blouse. The sight of the full swell of milky skin beneath a wisp of black lace forced a groan from him. "Lady, there's only one thing that can help me now."

She let her arms to drop to her sides. "Oh? And what might that be?"

He barely heard her words. Her luscious lips softened, sending him a silent invitation.

Incapable of refusing the sultry request, AJ gave in. He sank a hand into her hair, his fist clenching involuntarily around the silken curls. Ever so slowly, he tugged, pulling her head closer. His eyes fixed on her mouth, on the full upper lip as it parted from the lower one. The puff of air from her mouth warmed his and he inhaled it seconds before his lips touched hers.

Then her mouth was on his, applying a subtle, prohibited pressure. He groaned as her body curved into him. Four months he'd waited to taste her. Four months of hot dreams and cold showers. Her lips parted beneath his tongue and he allowed himself a languorous minute of exploration, discovering the hot, moist secrets she hid behind those succulent lips. She tasted like dessert, wine and imported chocolate. Sweet, with a touch of exotic spice. Cinnamon, perhaps.

Control, he reminded himself. *Lose control, you lose yourself.* He gave no more, holding himself rigid as her body sought to nestle into his. This had to be someone's idea of a sick joke. Testing him to see if he could taste her and walk away unscathed.

Impossible. She'd already touched a part of him no one else had reached in years. If she applied even the tiniest amount of effort, she'd be his undoing. Somehow, he knew, she had the power to overcome every obstacle he threw her way. She'd blast away his barriers and access the one part of his life he hadn't shared in a decade.

That couldn't happen. Ever. Pain that deep should not be shared.

His body paid no heed to his thoughts. It reacted on pure instinct. She wrapped her leg around his, pushed her hips up into his groin and ground herself against his cock.

Ah, crap. She wasn't making this easy.

As if sensing his reluctance, her arms crept around his neck and she clung. Her breasts pressed into his chest, the taut nipples a stark contradiction to the soft mounds beneath. She touched the tip of her tongue to his lower lip, compelling him to respond, to give as much as she could take.

For a nanosecond, he slackened his body and stilled his mouth against the erotic dance of her lips. Then four months of need and self-denial took over.

Blocking out his past, he groaned and hauled her against him, kissing her with the full, open-mouthed kiss she'd begged for. Her hot mouth curled his toes and flattened his resistance, rendering him powerless. He'd tasted her, and turning back ceased to be an option.

Desire rocketed through him, waking every tiny nerve ending. She moaned and the sound echoed through the elevator and, unfortunately, through his heart.

He dipped her backward, his arm supporting her lower back. Then he raked a hand down her chest, from the hollow in her neck to the deep "V" of her bra. The caress sent goosebumps rippling over her skin, and her back curved, propelling those incredible breasts upwards. Dazed by his need to taste them, he teased her blouse open, exposing her bra fully. His lips closed over the soft lace and he filled his mouth with the tip of a firm breast.

She gasped.

The sound gripped at his balls, yanking them tight beneath his cock. He suckled her and then nipped.

"Oh, God."

When at last he lifted his head and pulled her upright again, she said not a word, merely stared at him, her eyes brimming with victory and passion. Without releasing her, he reached out and pressed another button. The lift dinged three times and began to move.

"Your room," he said and registered vague surprise that he was coherent enough to form the words.

CR

Desire coursed through her, hastening her steps. He walked so close his breath stirred the hair on her neck. It didn't matter that she didn't know his name and had never seen him before today. It didn't matter that she'd probably never see him again. She wanted him tonight. Just for tonight, for one evening of potent, passionate pleasure.

Perhaps one night with him would be enough to stave off the persistent loneliness that cursed her. Enough to keep the yearning for a lover and partner at bay. A one-night stand in a hotel room was hardly the solution she sought, but a night with this sexy stranger was irresistible.

Primitive lust coursed through her. She hadn't intended to seduce him but when she'd found herself alone in the lift with him, instinct had taken over. His desire for her had been so obvious, she'd simply offered him a sample of that which he'd been eyeing.

With shaking hands, she opened the door to her room. Instinct told her this, them, was right. Whatever happened was meant to be. There'd be no regret the next morning, no allusions made to a future together. It would just be for tonight, and it would be good. Real good.

Although, a future together didn't seem altogether terrible.

He followed her in and kicked the door shut. Shrugging off his jacket and tie, he turned and pinned her between himself and the wall. Then he kissed her, reducing her to a shivering mass. Her legs refused to hold her upright any longer and she slid to the floor in a boneless heap.

The wall supported the sudden weight of her head, and tilting her neck she found herself at eye level with his pelvis. His suit pants clearly outlined his erection. Heat radiated from it. Leaning forward, she nuzzled her nose into his groin and grazed her teeth over his length. He shuddered.

"Easy," he breathed and dropped to his knees. "Let's make this last."

He nudged her thighs apart so he sat cradled between her legs. Angling her face upwards, he took her mouth in a steamy kiss. His lips stole reason, stole her breath, and she melted into him. She belonged to him. He could do whatever he wished.

She marveled at the instinctive trust she'd placed in a complete stranger. Something about him seemed safe. Secure. He wouldn't hurt her.

When he pulled his mouth away and leaned in to plant moist, warm kisses down her throat, she buried her nose in his soft hair. Triggers of awareness shot through her. If his mouth could seduce her without moving past her neck, what could he do to her when she lay naked beneath him?

Again, he kissed her lips. It started as a sweet, heady kiss, a slow exploration of a new pleasure. It quickly spiraled into a heated clash of lips, his mouth greedily sucking at hers. The action struck her deep within and her limbs tingled with pleasure. His hands flicked under her shirt, teasing the heated flesh beneath. A cool breeze against her hot skin told her he'd undone the clasp of her bra. He pushed her blouse over her shoulders but instead of removing it altogether, he caught the sleeves behind her back, snaring her hands, rendering her helpless.

He muttered something unintelligible and dropped his head to her chest. His warm breath on her nipples blew her mind. She shook uncontrollably and did something she'd never done before—begged him to touch her.

Fireworks exploded as his lips covered her nipple, as he sucked the engorged peak into his mouth. Oh, dear Lord, the man should give lessons in the art of kissing. His mouth tortured her with its practiced touch, his tongue took her to the edge of sanity and back. By the time he lifted his head to inhale deeply, he'd explored and discovered every inch of her chest.

Lexi trembled. His actions weren't just those of an anonymous lover. In his arms, she felt cherished. Needed. Secure. He made her feel sexy, too. She could do anything with him and she knew she'd be safe. She moaned mindlessly, her entire body shook and her breath came in short, sharp gulps. How could someone she'd just met stir such bone-deep emotion?

She watched him, watched as the frozen flames in his eyes absorbed her reaction to his touch. Once again, his devastating looks struck her dumb. Never mind the hard lines around his mouth and eyes. He took her breath away. There was more to him than just the fact that he was the sexiest man on earth. She sensed a depth behind his silence, a wealth of emotion behind his icy eyes.

"Please," she whispered. "I need to touch you." Her voice stunned her with its hoarseness. Something more than her physiological reaction to him was coming into play. Something more...intense.

He closed his eyes as a pained expression flashed across his face, and released her hands. Buttons flew across the room as she ripped his shirt open. She was a woman possessed. She had to touch him, had to see him.

As her eyes registered the sight before her, her hands froze mid-motion.

Muscle rippled down his chest to his waist. His stomach was hard and flat and she gawked at his sculpted torso. He had the kind of chest she could bury herself against. The kind of chest she wanted hanging around for, oh, about forever.

A dark smattering of hair dusted his chest, trailed down his belly and disappeared below his belt. Sweet Lord, she wanted to see what he kept hidden below that belt.

Leaning into him, she placed both hands on his chest and kissed him. She nudged him backward until he lay on the floor and she lay on top of him. Then she touched her tongue to the pulse throbbing at his throat. Salty. She licked lower. Hot. Her mouth settled above his nipple. It was tight and beaded and he groaned when she kissed it.

Ah, hell. Her panties were drenched. The more she nipped and licked, the wetter they got. She shimmied down him and ran her tongue over the grooves between each muscle, reveling in the reflexive contracting of his stomach. When she'd had her fill and his chest rose and fell unevenly, she slipped off him and undid his belt and pants. His cock jumped beneath her hands. She pulled back the waistband of his boxers, exposing the head of his dick.

"Christ, woman," he muttered. He lay dead still. Their eyes caught and held. His were dark, etched with hunger. Not a single trace of the coldness she'd seen in them earlier remained, only a flame of desire burning through the blue depths.

Exhilaration overcame her, making her smile. His resistance in the lift earlier had melted away. She dipped her head and a throaty growl erupted from his chest.

She licked at the pearly bead on the tip of his cock, swirled her tongue around and filled her mouth with his salty, male tang. His hands found her hair and the roots strained against her scalp as he reflexively tugged at her curls. She pushed at his pants until he shifted his hips and kicked off his shoes and the rest of his clothes, exposing a thick, hard cock and long, muscular legs covered with dark curls.

An unexpected surge of emotion washed over her as she

took in his nude form. She swallowed hard. This was supposed to be a night of gratuitous sex, nothing more. So why did something akin to affection well in her chest?

Giving herself a mental shake, she refocused her attention. She wrapped her hand around his shaft and lifted it slightly. From the tip of his cock, down his shaft and over his balls, she licked and sampled and nibbled, making her way over every delectable inch. He mumbled nonsensically, at which point she opened her lips wide and sucked him all in.

His control snapped. Before she knew it, he'd flipped her over. She lay on her back with him on top of her.

"I'm only human," he rasped and kissed her, hard. "I can take just so much teasing." He tugged at her skirt, pulled it up around her hips, and his hand found her panties. "So wet," he rumbled.

He nudged the lacy thong aside and found her hidden folds. They were moist with anticipation and she moaned as he skimmed over them.

"You like that?" He nudged her panties down and she shifted and kicked them off. Ever so lightly, he touched her clit.

"Oh, yes," she cried as he slid his finger down and rubbed it into her hot, wet slit. She'd have cried out his name, only she didn't know it.

"Good. Now let's see how much you can take." He slid his hand up again. Her breath came in short, sharp spurts as he repeated the movements in rhythmic sensuality.

Oh. My. God.

She opened her mouth to tell him how amazing it felt. At the same time, he pushed deep inside her and bit her nipple. The only sound she emitted was a loud "Aaaahhhh".

His tongue soothed her breast, easing the erotic sting, and

his hand conducted an orchestra of sensation deep within. He edged downwards until his mouth was directly above her groin. Hot breath whispered between her legs, and she shuddered.

When he darted out his tongue and licked her, he slid a second finger in.

Oh dear, dear, dear, sweet Lord.

Oh dear, dear, dear, sweet stranger.

His mouth devoured her. His deep strokes within compounded the tension. He was good—so damn good, and she could not contain the orgasm that swept over her. She came, her entire body swamped with convulsions of pleasure.

She was still reeling when he reached up and kissed her mouth. She tasted herself on his lips, and her groin clenched in reaction. She shook from the aftermath of her orgasm, but emptiness seized her. Something was missing.

That something nudged her upper thigh. She shifted so the head of his cock brushed her ultra-sensitive lips. Her legs bent instinctively as she prepared to take him in.

"Wait," he rasped as she rubbed her clit against him, need flooding through her.

Christ, she couldn't wait another second. She wanted him inside, now.

"I need a condom."

As he rifled through his pants and wallet, she dipped her hand down. She needed his cock inside her. He was taking too damn long. Her eyes closed as she touched herself.

Her swollen bud responded instantly. She stroked herself, imaging her hand was his. As good as it felt, it wasn't enough. She delved between her lips, explored as deeply as she could and moaned. Because it was good. But still not good enough.

"Not enough," she groaned out loud. "Not enough."

"Jesus."

She opened her eyes. He stared at her, frozen. His cock was half-sheathed in a condom. She pulled her finger out, only to slide it in again. Her wanton behavior shocked and excited her. She was fucking herself in front of him, and the more she did it the faster his breath came.

It was good, but...

"Not enough," she panted.

He was on top of her. Her arms were pinned at her sides and he was driving into her. His thick, beautiful cock pushing into her, stretching her, filling her. Completing her.

She screamed as he filled her to the hilt. "Yes. Oh, God yes." She was beyond caring about her totally unrestrained and uninhibited behavior. All she cared about was him, pushing into her, driving her past reality and into a realm where sensation alone existed.

"Fuck me," she cried, and he did.

Tingling burst into full-blown raptures, her muscles clamped down around him and she convulsed again. Waves of pleasure rolled through her for a second incredible time.

Sanity returned and the tremors passed slowly. His eyes were squeezed shut, his body frozen and his shoulders taut with the effort of remaining still.

She wrapped her legs around his waist and rolled her hips.

Sweat beaded on his forehead as he fought to keep her movements in check. She rolled her hips again. With a fierce groan, he let go of his restraint. He pulled out and thrust back in again, hard and fast, and then did it again and again. Coming so close on the heels of her orgasm, the friction against her inner walls sent her over the top. She cried out at the mad sensations swirling through her. It was too much. She'd never experienced anything like it before, she was too sensitive, she couldn't...

Oh, sweet heaven, yes, she could. She was going to. Again. This time, he was coming with her. She clenched her muscles around him and he cried out in response.

"Lexi," he rasped and gave up all pretence at control. He plunged into her repeatedly, his movements wild and uninhibited, and she met him thrust for thrust. He stretched her and filled her and enticed her and wowed her, and the tension built, higher and higher. As her body gave way to the third and most powerful set of spasms yet, he gave one last thrust, his body stiffened and he cried out her name and joined her as she tilted over the edge of reason and into a whirlpool of pleasure.

Passionate, potent pleasure.

AJ lay in her bed longer than he should have. Her head rested on his shoulder and her breast was squashed against his chest. After the night they'd shared, wanting her again should have been a physical impossibility. His dick disagreed. The first stirrings of arousal prickled his belly.

He suppressed a groan and carefully, so as not to wake her, disentangled his body from hers. Slipping from the sheets tortured him. His heart objected immediately—unexpected pangs of regret tightened his ribs.

Christ, what had he done?

Broken his own cardinal rule, that's what. He'd slept with the one woman he'd vowed to keep at a distance. The one woman he feared had the ability to break through his barriers and access his secret. His terrible, tragic secret.

He dressed quickly, knowing if he remained naked any longer, desire would beat down his need for control. He'd caress her exposed breast, kiss her into wakefulness and lose himself once more in her bewitching charms.

The sun peaked through the curtains. Time to leave. At least under cover of night he could pretend their encounter had been meaningless. Facing her in the clear light of day would be too stark a reminder of what he'd risked.

Once before he'd put his heart on the line and the experience had destroyed him. He'd vowed never again to chance such utter devastation. If he never allowed himself the weakness of emotion, he'd be just fine.

Lexi Tanner had the power to evoke powerful emotions in him. Not love, mind you. Such sentiment no longer interested him. As things stood, he barely got through a day without constant, painful reminders of the cost of love. It wasn't the idea of falling for Lexi that scared him shitless—he knew it could never happen. It was the knowledge that given half a chance he'd let her in. He'd be unable to resist. She'd tunnel her way into his life and into his past, and she'd make him feel again.

That was something AJ did not want to do.

His shirt hung open—the only button still attached dangled uselessly on a thread. He shrugged on his jacket and mentally coerced his growing erection down. Shit, just thinking about their night got him hot.

It was a damn good thing he'd never see her again. Last night he'd relinquished control. He could never risk that kind of vulnerability again. In the future, he would avoid Lexi at all costs.

Chapter Three

When Lexi awoke, he was gone.

At some point during the night they'd moved to the bed, and with him curled protectively around her, Lexi had fallen into an exhausted, satisfied sleep. When she'd opened her eyes a few hours later and stretched her deliciously aching limbs over the soft mattress, she found herself alone.

The crumpled sheets and her scattered clothes bore testimony to the fact that she had not dreamed up the previous night. The warm glow in her belly confirmed the reality. What a reality—better than any fantasy she might have had.

Christ, the man had been insatiable. So had she. He'd made her come three times in the space of half an hour and then at least another six times during the night. Each time, she'd thought he'd wrenched the last orgasm from her. Then somehow he'd manage to inspire another one.

She'd wanted a little pleasure with him and she'd gotten it. Repeatedly. On the floor, on the chair, in the shower—and the bath—and finally, in the bed.

She stretched again and yawned, and a strong, pleasant smell reached her nose. His scent mingled with the smell of sex. Strong masculine smells that fired her imagination and her body. Her thighs ached and muscles she never knew she had were stiff from the night's vigorous workout.

Heavens, she could do with a workout like that at least every day.

Now he was gone and real life continued. Sighing, she forced herself out of bed and into the shower. She waited for the water to heat, then adjusted the pressure so the jets pulsated over her tender body, washing away the sticky remains of their passion.

Last night had been unforgettable. He'd turned a night of casual, anonymous sex into something spectacular. Perhaps she had broken through her usual limitations and surrendered herself to whatever he'd suggested because the night had been shrouded in anonymity. She'd done things with him she'd never dreamed of doing with another man. Far from embarrassing her, it had liberated her. Their sex had affected her on a primal and emotional level. It had filled her and fulfilled her and left her more complete today than she had been in a very long time.

It also left her emptier than she had been in a long time. Last night she hadn't intended to get emotionally involved. It was all supposed to have been about sex. When she'd least expected it, she'd experienced...something. She wasn't sure what. Just...something. Which only served to exacerbate her loneliness this morning.

She washed her hair, taking a long time to work the shampoo into a rich lather, massaging her scalp languorously, her arms too relaxed to move any faster

He'd been affected just as deeply. She'd seen it in his eyes, in the melting of the ice-blue irises as passion suffused him. She'd seen it in his mouth, in the softening of the hard lines after he'd kissed her. In the lusty groans he'd emitted when she'd surrendered to him and to the pleasure that his touch provoked. She'd felt it in his arms, in the way he'd held her afterwards like a fragile bird.

The strong scent of the chamomile-vanilla conditioner filled her nose, overshadowing the last traces of the male fragrance that had clung to her skin. Now all she had left of him was her memories. Memories of a beautiful, nameless man, a glorious, gratifying night and magnificent sex.

She rinsed the soap from her body, switched off the water and climbed out of the shower. As she toweled herself dry, patting down the places where just a few hours before his lips and hands had been, a dizzying mix of melancholy and relief settled over her. He was gone and she'd never see him again.

CR

"He's what?" She stared at the woman, aghast.

"He's checked out," the woman repeated.

"Oh...when?" Lexi asked, stupefied.

"This morning. At about seven-thirty."

Seven-thirty. Around the same time she'd been washing away the last remnants of her stranger from her body.

Damn it. The newspaper article had said Riley would be at the hotel for four days, and she'd only read it yesterday. How could he have left already? She hadn't had a chance to speak to him yet.

"Please, I need to see him. It's urgent," she tried again.

"I'm sorry, miss. He's left. I simply cannot help you."

"I...oh...um...I... Never mind. Thanks for your help." Lexi's shoulders slumped in defeat.

She'd blown it. She'd had a fighting chance to track down Riley and get him to listen, and she'd blown it. He'd gone and checked out while she'd daydreamed in the shower. Okay, so the daydreams were worth spending a little time over, but now she had no idea where Riley might be.

Not that it mattered. She was flying back to Sydney this evening anyway, after the close of the conference. She'd have to wait until her official appointment on Wednesday to see him.

Chapter Four

Five minutes before her appointment on Wednesday afternoon, Lexi stepped into an elevator in the Riley Building. She checked her appearance in the mirror, straightened her collar and smoothed down an invisible wrinkle on her blouse.

She was about to meet AJ Riley. After six weeks of waiting and restless impatience, she would finally get to talk to him and—she hoped—finally get the desperately needed money so she could put it to good use.

Tucked in her briefcase were pages of useful stats, books and articles and a detailed proposal of her project. Riley should know she wasn't starting up the program on an emotional whim. She'd done extensive research and had enough facts and figures to more than justify the cost of the set-up.

She needed to blow Mr. Riley away. By the time she left his office, he had to be just as convinced of the merits of the project as she was.

Lexi stood alone in the lift as it glided to the top floor of probably the highest building in the city. She shivered. Since the conference, she hadn't been able to view elevators in the same way. They were no longer just a means of getting from one floor to the next. Now they were tiny, intimate rooms where delicious acts of seduction took place.

For the gazillionth time in three days, she relived that night in her head. She felt his hands on her breasts and his mouth between her legs. By the time the doors slid open, she was flushed and her panties were more than a little damp.

Walking into Riley's office with glazed eyes and a major nipple stand probably wouldn't be the best way to make a professional first impression.

She fanned her face, collected her thoughts and focused on the task ahead. Her stomach trembled from a sudden case of nerves. If she couldn't convince Riley of the brilliance of the sibling program, she wouldn't get the money from him.

Dear God, she needed his donation. If Riley didn't come through, she might not be able to start the project.

His secretary's office left her with no doubt that Riley had spent a small fortune on furniture and art. Beautiful paintings hung on the walls. On one side of the room, a glass and cherrywood coffee table framed an expensive-looking Persian rug and navy leather couches trimmed its edges.

On the other side, a capable-looking woman of forty-plus sat behind a matching cherrywood desk. Genevieve, Riley's secretary. The only person with whom Lexi had had any contact from Riley Corporation.

"May I help you?" she asked.

"Lexi Tanner. I'm here to see AJ Riley."

"His four o'clock." Genevieve nodded and motioned Lexi to the leather couches. "Please take a seat, I'll let him know you've arrived."

Lexi sat, watching as the woman knocked on, and then disappeared behind, a huge oak door. Anticipation hummed in her veins. This was it. Almost seven weeks of waiting were up.

What would Riley be like?

Domineering and to the point? Kind and gentle? Unfocused and occupied with other matters? Would he smooth down his moustache while he listened? Remove his glasses when he spoke?

Would he even be interested in what she had to say?

"Miss Tanner?" She hadn't noticed Genevieve return. "Mr. Riley will see you now." She showed Lexi into his office and shut the door behind her.

A panoramic view through two enormous corner windows almost bowled Lexi over. It was uninterrupted across the city, over the bridge and onto the North Shore. From where she stood, she could see the ferries gliding past the Opera House and into Circular Quay.

Riley sat at his desk in a high-backed, black leather chair, facing the window. If not for the phone cord stretching from desk to chair, she wouldn't have known he was in the office at all. He spoke to someone—or listened, rather, as Lexi didn't hear him say anything.

She took a minute to look around his office.

His desk was made from the same wood that had been used in his secretary's office. It dominated the room. Leather-bound volumes of books filled a matching bookshelf. Another expensive-looking rug covered the floor, and more beautiful paintings framed the walls. She recognized each of them as originals and it came as a surprise to find she and Riley shared a similar taste in art. The difference? She had to make do with prints.

The office was neat and ordered. From the sleek Mac on his desk to the glass-doored wall unit across the room, everything appeared spick-and-span. It also shouted out *control freak*. There was not a paper to be seen, not a pen lying around. Everything had its place and, quite obviously, everything was in its place.

Not particularly wanting to stand around like an idiot, she took a seat in a matching chair on the opposite side of his desk. Lexi didn't consider herself short yet the chair engulfed her. Was that a business strategy he used? Making people feel small in his office?

Ridiculous. His chair was the same size as hers. Now that she concentrated, she realized the seat did not hide Riley completely. She could see the top of his head. Her first glimpse of the man.

He was tall—he had to be if his head was sticking out—and maybe not as old as she'd originally thought. She'd expected his hair to be a silvery grey. Quite the contrary, it was dark as sin and looked thick and luxurious—much like her stranger's had been.

She idly wondered what it would be like to run her fingers through it. Would it have the same silky texture as *his* had?

Don't even go there. She was here to ask him for money. Thinking about stroking his hair hardly seemed appropriate.

The proposal. She'd take it out and be prepared to launch into discussion as soon as he put down the phone. As she retrieved it from her bag, something about the air in his office gave her pause for thought, and she stopped and inhaled deeply.

A familiar scent teased her nose. It had since she'd first stepped inside. She recognized it, although she wasn't sure where from. The subtle, masculine fragrance permeated her senses and tugged at her mind and at her chest, enticing her to recall a memory that was just out of reach. Her body stirred, responding to the sultry scent. So much for suppressing the nipple stand.

She stared sightlessly ahead, lost in thought, trying to

place the memory. A sense of longing filled her. Her longtime companion, loneliness, returned, as strong as it had been in Melbourne the morning after. The scent filled her nose, familiar and alluring, making that emptiness seem a million times worse.

"What about the Lewin Deal?" Riley asked into the phone, yanking Lexi's attention back to the office.

His voice was low, deep and throaty, and the second he spoke she knew she'd heard it before. She also knew she'd never expected to hear it again. The air in the office seemed to thin and Lexi found breathing difficult.

Inhale.

Her lungs constricted and oxygen couldn't fill them fast enough. The blood drained from her face, her stomach dropped into her knees and she gripped the arms of the chair so tight her knuckles went into spasm.

Oh. Dear. God.

"Fine, make it Tuesday." *Fine. Let's do it.*

Miniscule bumps shivered up her neck. It wasn't possible.

"Good. See you then." He swiveled his chair around and hung up.

Bizarrely, her first thought upon seeing his face was that AJ Riley didn't have a moustache after all. Or glasses, for that matter.

Unmistakable ice-blue eyes appraised her. "Miss Tanner, I presume?" His tone was mocking and cold, not warm and honeyed like she remembered. His mouth was set in grim lines, harsh and unforgiving, not full and swollen from her kisses. His eyes were distant and condescending, not heated and hungry like before.

"You!" The word ripped through her throat. Disbelief

echoed in her ears.

Her nameless lover was AJ Riley?

"You were expecting someone else?" he scoffed.

Shock rendered her speechless. She'd slept with AJ Riley. After weeks of unsuccessful attempts to track him down, she'd unwittingly slept with him.

"You seem surprised," he commented dispassionately.

She gaped at him. Surprised? Flabbergasted, more like it. Gobsmacked, astounded and dumbfounded to boot. Not to mention thrown so far off balance the entire office block spun.

She hadn't just slept with the man—she'd fucked him senseless. Now what the hell was she supposed to do? She was never meant to see him again. The pure anonymity of their encounter had led her to do things with him she'd never have done under ordinary circumstances. She'd masturbated in front of him—touched herself, fucked herself. Shamelessly begged him to fuck her.

Now she sat across from him in his office, about to beg again. Only this time it was for money. Nausea rose in her stomach. She did the math and, for once, one and one did not make two. It added up to her looking like a whore.

Spots danced before her eyes and she prayed she wouldn't pass out. She'd embarrassed herself in front of him enough already.

"Do you plan on saying anything, Miss Tanner, or should I attempt to infer from your body language your reasons for being here?"

Cold. He was so cold. So distant. Not to mention rude. The man she'd made love with hadn't been like this. How could she blame him? If she thought she looked like a whore, she could only imagine what he thought. Trying in vain to pull her thoughts together, she straightened her back and considered what to say.

Something else bothered her, something other than her complete and utter humiliation.

"I believe," he prompted her, "you are here to ask for a donation?"

She tried to focus on his words. What bothered her? It was there, trapped somewhere in her subconscious. If she could just access it...

Think, Tanner.

"Would you care to tell me a little about your...needs?"

There was no mistaking the innuendo in his question. He knew all about her...needs.

His tone made it obvious he wasn't the least bit interested in her cause, in the real reason she was here. It was aloof and expressionless. It didn't sound at all like it had in her hotel room. Then it had been warm and sensual. When he'd whispered his carnal wishes in her ear, it had been low and roughened by desire. When he'd lost himself in the throws of a wild orgasm and called out her name, it had been hoarse and hot and completely unrestrained. When...

Oh, Jesus. That was it.

He'd called out her name. She'd thought he hadn't known her identity...but he'd screamed her name. *"Lexi"*.

Red-hot fury pulsed through her. Maybe she used it as a weapon to hide her embarrassment. Maybe she was just pissed off about being misled. Whatever the reason, she was livid. All the warm, content feelings she'd had about their night together rocketed out the window. How could he? How the fuck could he have done that?

She surged to her feet, her movement so fast and fierce she

knocked the chair over. It landed with a resounding crash on the carpeted floor. Much the way she wished her fist could smash into his nose.

"You bastard," she spat at him. "You cold, callous bastard." She knew her cheeks flamed. She flamed, so angry she could barely see straight.

"You knew all along, didn't you?" She kicked the chair out of the way—no mean feat, considering its size—and banged her fists on the desk. Pens scattered from his ever-so-pristine penholder and clattered down on the polished cherrywood. She fervently hoped one had gouged a sizeable mark out of his immaculate desk.

"You knew exactly who I was, right from that first moment in the lobby, didn't you?"

He assessed her with cold eyes. "Of course I did. Do you think I'd sleep with someone I don't know?"

She gaped at him. "You knew who I was and you never had the decency to tell me? You slept with me without so much as hinting at your familiarity?"

The corner of his mouth turned up. She'd never describe the expression as pleasant. "And I suppose you didn't know who I was?" He tossed out the idea with a dismissive wave of his hand. "Impossible. You made this appointment weeks ago. You knew exactly who I was. Didn't you, Lexi?"

"How could I?" she snarled. "I'd never met you. Until one minute ago, I didn't even know what AJ Riley looked like."

"Oh, you knew," he taunted. "And you took full advantage of our unexpected meeting at the hotel. It was quite perfect, wasn't it? Seduce me first to butter me up, and then ask for money."

"You weren't buttered, you were creamed," she retorted, remembering the sight of her juices coating his cock and his mouth.

Oh... Crap. Had she just said that out loud?

"And what tasty cream it was," he said, licking his lips thoughtfully.

For just a moment, she caught a glimpse of the lover he'd been in Melbourne, and not the bastard sitting across the desk. He might as well have kissed her between the legs, with the animalistic way her body reacted to the motion.

He eyed her groin openly. "Care to offer me another sample before we get down to business? It might tempt me to give you the money you so obviously need."

For the first time ever, Lexi experienced a sudden urge to strangle someone, to put her hands around his throat and choke the last breath out of him. She wasn't sure what pissed her off more. His malicious insinuations, or the fact that she was seriously turned on by the idea of him going down on her again. The combination of anger and arousal made her so hot, she knew she'd go off like a machine gun the second his mouth touched her. Which it never would.

Wait. She was here to discuss the sibling program, not fantasize about fucking him. Or killing him, for that matter. As enraged as she was, the kids had to come first. She had to put her thoughts and emotions aside and focus on her objective.

With as much decorum as she could muster, she looked him dead in the eye. "Contrary to what you might believe, I did not sleep with you for money. Had I known from the start who you were, things would never have...taken the turn they did. As it stands, I have to deal with the repercussions of my impulsivity, and trust me, that is no easy task. If you could see fit to put the night behind us and move on, I would be most grateful."

He didn't bat an eyelid. "So why did you sleep with me?"

"Pardon?"

"If you didn't sleep with me for money, why did you sleep with me?"

Why the fuck did he think she'd slept with him? Because she couldn't keep her hands off him, that's bloody why.

"Mr. Riley, please. The night was what it was. Nothing more, nothing less. No hidden agendas, no unspoken needs. I hid nothing from you, because I didn't know who you were. Now, about the pro—"

"You wouldn't be the first, you know? To use sex for money."

Why, of all the arrogant, assholish things to say. Now she didn't just feel like a whore, she felt like a common whore—just as he'd intended. The rage she'd suppressed minutes ago bubbled menacingly in her stomach. She tried, she *really* tried, but a woman could gather only so much patience before losing it altogether.

Think of the kids. "About the project, Mr. Riley..."

"Was it worth it? Prostituting yourself like that?"

Acid burned her gut. *The siblings. It's all for them, don't forget them.*

Then, as if he really were just curious, he said, "Do you make it a habit? Sleeping with the people you're about to request a donation from?"

She blew up. "Fuck you, you arrogant, twisted asshole. Fuck you and the chariot you rode in on."

"Temper, temper, Miss Tanner."

Loathing coursed through her. "'Miss Tanner'?" she hissed. "You were screaming out my name just a few short days ago and now you feel the need for formalities?"

As if unaffected by her outburst, his voice dropped to the

husky tone that had driven her wild. "As I recall it, I wasn't the only one screaming. Lexi."

Her name came out as a purr and she felt it like a soft caress against her skin. Unbelievable. The man had her livid as she'd ever been, and she was turned on. Un-bloody-believable.

"Yeah," she agreed, the irrepressible urge to kill him surfacing once again. "I screamed. Does it turn you on? The thought of paying a woman to scream when she fucks you? Do you have other preferences? You know, things women will only do for you for money?"

A small voice in the back of her head reminded her that no matter what else happened, she was still in his office as a representative of the hospital. Hurling profanities at him wasn't exactly professional behavior.

Oh please. He'd watched her jam her fingers up her vagina. Swearing at him now was hardly going to tarnish her professional image.

"A lot of things turn me on, Lexi. Paying a woman to sleep with me isn't one of them."

Darn, did he have to keep repeating her name in that sleep-with-me voice? "And yet you seemed pretty turned on when you thought you were sleeping with me for money."

He merely lifted an eyebrow. "Or maybe I knew money would never enter the equation."

"You have a...a...I...oh." Oh! His words penetrated her fury.

He wasn't going to sponsor the sibling program. She'd argued the semantics of him paying her to sleep with him, and he'd never had any intention of giving her money in the first place.

Oh. Bugger. All her efforts, all her energies, all the time she'd focused on him. Wasted. He'd known who she was and what she wanted all along, and he'd never intended to sponsor the project.

The fight drained out of her. Before she'd even had a chance to present her case, she'd lost it. She wouldn't receive the necessary funding from Riley Corporation. Riley wasn't interested.

The sibling program was doomed.

The thought of spending another minute in his company suddenly exhausted her. She had to get the hell out of his office. Her humiliation was too great a burden to bear in public. In the space of a few minutes, he'd not only rejected her project—the work that meant more to her than anything else she'd ever attempted—he'd also effectively killed every beautiful memory of their night together.

He'd taken their spectacular lovemaking and turned it into nothing more than a cheap, dirty affair. To top it all, her body was still fiercely aware of him, of his masculinity and his presence. Still nudging her subconscious to sleep with him again. Begging her self-conscious. Talk about adding insult to injury—betrayed by her own body.

She had to get away. Using every ounce of energy and dignity she possessed, which, considering the circumstances, was not very much, she straightened the chair she'd knocked over.

Her sense of gloom and humiliation mingled with a need for self-preservation, and as she replaced the papers she'd removed from her briefcase, she looked at Riley. "Just for the record," she told him, "I slept with a stranger in Melbourne. Someone I'd never laid eyes on before. Our meeting today was my first opportunity to see what AJ Riley looked like."

"You're asking me to believe that you had no idea who I was?" The lines around his mouth tightened.

"Believe whatever you want, Mr. Riley." She no longer possessed the energy to care.

"You knew. I saw the recognition in your eyes as soon as you looked up at me in the lobby."

"Recognition? I didn't rec—" Lexi snapped her mouth shut. Riley was half right. She had recognized something then. Only it wasn't his identity. It was her immediate, overwhelming attraction to him.

She'd hardly grant him the satisfaction of telling him that now. "I repeat—I had no idea who you were." She closed her bag and prepared to leave. She'd go out looking like a professional, not like some two-bit whore. "Now, if you'll excuse me, the time has come for me to leave. I'm afraid I made a grave error of judgment coming here today, and I apologize for wasting your time." Her voice sounded eerily normal. "I'll show myself out."

"You're leaving?" he asked, and even looked a little surprised.

"Apparently my expectations of our eventual meeting were unrealistic. I find you're not...quite the man I thought you to be, and it's obvious you want no part in the sibling program. There's really no point in my taking up any more of your day." She walked to the door. "Goodbye, Mr. Riley. It's been...a real delight getting to know you at last."

AJ, you can be a real asshole when you want to.

He hauled a hand through his hair and shook his head. Sure, he'd needed to get Lexi the hell out of his office, and out of his life, but damn, did he have to act like such a dickhead in the process? Why didn't he just politely refer her to Matt, who usually dealt with charities and donations anyway?

Because, he admitted to himself, Lexi Tanner scared the crap out of him.

If he'd thought spending a night with her could cure his eternal hard-on, he'd been sadly mistaken. Sleeping with the woman had the exact opposite effect. Instead of getting her out of his system, she plagued him. He spent every available second consumed by thoughts of her. Not just images of her naked— although those did take up a substantial amount of time—images of her fully dressed, drinking coffee, eating dinner, having a bath, working, shopping, swimming, sleeping, waking, walking, standing blah, blah, blah.

Worst of all, he imagined her sitting with her feet curled under her legs on the lounger on the balcony of his holiday home, talking. To him. Because Lexi made him want to do that. To sit cozily in his house and just spend time with her.

AJ did not take the time to get to know the women he had sex with. If one pleased him, he saw her again. If she didn't, he didn't. Simple. End of story. Lexi didn't just please him. She fascinated him. Inspired him. Sent his thoughts skittering to the proverbial family home with the white picket fence and the two-point-five children.

That's why he'd sent her the hell away. He wasn't interested in any of it. Least of all the white picket fence and two-point-five children.

For fuck sake, Riley. Why'd ya have to go and be such a jerk?

Because she knew who I was. She knew all along.

Bullshit. She didn't have a clue.

'Course she did. Soon as Genevieve told me about the appointment when I got back, I put it all together. She set the whole thing up. Realized we were at the same hotel and thought she'd give me a little early incentive, so to speak.

Rubbish, she's not the type.

Sure she is. She recognized me in the lobby.

She recognized you in your office. Didn't you get a look at her face?

She's a good actress.

She was blown away.

She set me up.

Keep telling yourself that. I'm sure it helps.

It does.

Good.

It really does.

I'm happy for you.

I feel way better.

I'm sure she does too.

Ah, crap.

AJ jumped up and took off for the lift. Maybe he could catch her before she left. "Lexi," he yelled as he tore past Genevieve's desk.

"What on..." The door slammed behind him, cutting off the rest of his secretary's stunned question.

"Lexi, wait." He reached the elevators in time to see the doors closing. "Damn it, Lexi, wait." Shoving his hand through the microscopic gap, he prayed to God it didn't get mashed to a bloody pulp. As the doors touched his skin, he let rip with a steady stream of uninhibited cursing.

Much to his relief, the doors slid open again in the nick of time, leaving his hand very much intact. He marched into the lift and found her eyeing him cautiously. She eased the pressure off the *door open* button and hit *G*.

He hit *door open*. Christ, she was beautiful. Even though

loathing radiated from her in waves, she took his breath away. He wanted to touch her again. Needed to touch her. So he attacked instead.

"Spell it out, Lexi," he demanded as a nasty pounding began above his right eye. "What kind of game are you playing?"

"I don't play games, Mr. Riley," she told him through clenched teeth. "I outgrew that kind of behavior a long time ago." She hit *G*.

He held down *door open*. "Then what exactly are you doing here?" Shit, he better not be getting a migraine.

"You know what I'm doing here. I came to approach Riley Corporation for a donation. Now I've changed my mind. No matter how determined I am to set up this program, I will not prostitute myself for your money."

Pain shot up his neck and into his skull. She hadn't prostituted herself. She hadn't had the foggiest idea who he was. He knew it. "Look, can we talk, please? Contrary to what I may have implied, I actually am interested in the project. I'd like to put money toward it."

She smiled grimly and shook her head. "Thank you. Your money is no longer required. Now if you could remove your hand, I need to get down to the ground floor."

AJ nodded and pressed *G*. "Please," he said as the lift began to descend, "don't make any rash decisions. Hear me out first." He had to sit down before his skull exploded and tiny bits of brain splattered the walls of the lift.

"My decision is not rash. After careful thought, I've come to the conclusion that a night of shady sex would not be a solid foundation to base a children's support group."

"Shady sex?" he roared, then regretted it instantly as pain whipped down his forehead and over his eye. "You think that's—"

The lift bumped to a stop and the doors opened. A man stepped inside.

"Lift's full," AJ barked. "Take the next one." He banged on the *door close* button, and the startled passenger jumped out backward as the doors shut again. If Lexi thought she'd get away with describing their night together as shady...

"What is with you?" she snapped. "Throwing testosterone around like some kind of an animal. Are you on a mission to insult everyone you speak to today? Or is this some kind of twisted attempt to trap me in a lift alone with you? Again?"

Okay, so she was as aware of the irony of their surroundings as he was. It didn't help his head any.

"Was once not enough?" she seethed. "Is this how you prove your male domination? By trapping unsuspecting women in elevators?"

"Just one woman," he corrected her. "And you knew exactly what was coming." And damned if it wasn't going to come again. Yeah, she may be all fired up and pissed off. She was also turned on. He'd spent enough intimate time with her to recognize the look in her eyes when she became aroused. Besides, her nipples were hard beads poking through her shirt.

She glowered at him with smoky, hooded eyes.

A fine trickle of perspiration ran down his spine. He had a hard-on and a killer headache, and he wasn't sure which hurt more.

She bit her lower lip.

"Shit, woman," he gasped and backed her into the wall. Before she had a chance to resist, he kissed her.

There was nothing tender about his kiss. It was brutal, dragging a response from her even as she beat her fists against his arms. He didn't want to relish the jolt of desire in his stomach, or the now familiar pull in his chest. Her resistance appealed even less. He increased the intensity of the kiss, pushing his tongue past her lips, rediscovering the velvety depth of her mouth.

Although her wild flailing continued, her punches weakened until she no longer hit him at all. Instead, she grabbed at him. First his arms and then his waist, and then his hips.

He didn't want to respond to her. He didn't want to feel anything, except maybe her naked body against his. His head throbbed. He should just have stayed the hell away from her.

No, he shouldn't have.

Her hands found his ass and molded themselves to it as her mouth hungrily responded to his. This was no loving kiss. This was a fierce battle of wills. Neither of them wanted to be there, neither could stay away. Her tongue tortured his mouth with its violent counterattack. Nothing had felt as good in three long days.

He wasn't close enough. Had to get closer, had to pull her, full length, against him. She beat him to it. Grabbing his shoulders, she shimmied against the wall and, using them both for leverage, hoisted her hips up to meet his as she wrapped her legs around his waist.

Better. At least now she was massaging herself on his cock. She rocked against him and he thickened and grew beneath her movements. She groaned into his mouth and he responded by nicking her tongue with his teeth.

The layers of clothing between them only heightened his sense of the forbidden. He shouldn't be doing this. She was trouble. The thought didn't stop him from kissing her. She was aroused and he was hard, and she was bucking wildly against him, making soft mewling sounds that echoed in his stomach and his heart.

God help him, she had him so hot, so aroused, that if they carried on this way, he'd lose it right here in the slowly descending lift. Fully clothed.

Even as he thought it, her legs stiffened around him. She cried out, stilled completely, and just like that, she climaxed.

Her body shuddered and shook in his arms, and she panted in his ear, the warm uneven puffs of air tickling his neck. He held her tight as she slowed to erratic shivers, knowing that if she groaned so much as once, he'd come too. He was so close. So bloody close. There was little to no chance of holding out. Hearing her voice her satisfaction would do him in completely.

Focus on the headache. Suffer the pain. It was a vague tickle compared to the throbbing in his cock.

The lift dinged.

Her horrified gasp gave him the control he so desperately needed.

"Close your eyes," he ordered as common sense returned in a rush. "Relax your neck, drop your head back and for Christ sake, trust me."

By the time the doors slid open to reveal the ground floor of the building, Lexi lay seemingly unconscious in his arms, her face hot and her breathing irregular.

"She just needs some air," Riley said as he began to walk, his steps fast and purposeful. "Give me some space and I'll get her outside. She'll be fine."

Just as well he carried her, because the orgasm had ripped through her from nowhere. One minute she was frantically rubbing against him, desperate to have him inside her, and the next she was convulsing madly around his waist before collapsing, once again, in a boneless heap in his arms.

If her life had depended on it, she couldn't have walked out of the lift.

Oh, God. How could she lose it like that? What was the matter with her? He'd called her a whore, for heaven's sake. He'd treated her like one. How had she responded? She'd gone and behaved like one.

With one kiss, she'd come apart at the seams.

Except it wasn't just the kiss.

There was something about AJ Riley. No matter what other emotions he evoked in her—extreme rage or warm content— when he was around, a savage, sexual hunger besieged her. A hunger only he could sate.

A rush of air hit her. They were outside. She opened one eye and looked at him, aware her face must be a thousand different shades of purple.

"You okay?" he asked. The timbre of his voice was warm honey and liquid sex, and she simply could not respond.

He walked to a shadowed alcove. "I'm going to put you down now," he warned and the hot honey dripped over her skin.

She shuddered.

"I'm going to put you down," he repeated unnecessarily and didn't move.

He simply held her and she simply let him.

Until she realized she must weigh a ton and shifted in his arms.

Carefully, he removed his arm from beneath her knees, the same arm with which he held her briefcase, and she eased her feet to the ground. He kept his other arm behind her back, so the only way she could maneuver herself into an upright position without knocking them both over was to slide down his body.

Dear Lord, he was still just as hard as he'd been in the lift—and she was just as flustered. She tilted her head and looked up at him, found herself drowning in his blue eyes. "Mr. Riley, I—"

"Adam."

She was floored. "What?"

"My name," he said and smiled. "It's Adam. Not Riley or AJ or Mr. Riley. Just Adam."

For a full minute, she couldn't breathe. The smile lit both his face and the shadowed alcove where they stood. It thawed the ice in his eyes and in her heart. She could have stared at it all day because it was just so damn sexy.

"Adam," she repeated stupidly. He had the kind of smile that stopped cars. If anyone else saw it, Sydney would be caught in the worst traffic jam in history.

He hid his face from the rest of the world and focused his expression solely on her. Lexi stood transfixed, trapped against the hard length of his body.

"Adam," she said again.

He took a deep breath. "It would seem, Lexi, that today's meeting started out on the wrong foot."

Crap, there he went again, saying her name like it was a lover's caress or something.

"There's a little restaurant just across the road." He motioned behind him. "Will you join me for a coffee? Maybe we can start again. On the right foot this time."

Because he smiled as he said it, and kept his arm on her back, she walked beside him without argument as he made his way across the road and into the coffee shop.

Chapter Five

Adam watched Lexi pull some sheets from her briefcase and bite on her lower lip. That little habit of hers would be the death of him. It was totally provocative and elicited a bone-deep response from him. It should be his lip she chewed, not her own.

He wanted her. So bad, he considered tossing the coffee out of the way, hauling her across the table, onto his lap, and possessing her mouth again. That way, at least, he could hold her sweet butt against his cock, which was still rigid and demanding the release he'd ruthlessly suppressed in the elevator.

The pressure did little to relieve the pain of his headache.

His thoughts stretched back to Melbourne. He couldn't stop them. Their night together had been the most intense experience he'd had in a decade. The sex had been amazing but it wasn't the only part that had gotten to him. She'd given herself to him completely, held nothing back. As a result, he'd done the same.

Which was a bit of a shocker really, because he never let go. Not with anyone.

When he'd woken to find her spooned against him, still asleep, his gut had churned with emotion he wasn't ready to acknowledge. Lexi represented everything he no longer believed in. She embodied life and love and hope, and it vibrated through him, straight to that dark place in his heart. That place where hope had died long ago.

He hadn't been able to deal with it. He hadn't wanted to. So he'd come home to Sydney and left Matt behind to complete the business deal. Back at the office, Genevieve had dealt the killer blow. She told him about the appointment.

Two major thoughts had dominated: One—he'd wanted to see her again as much as he hadn't wanted to. And two—she'd known who he was all along. Both thoughts had been hell to deal with. He should have cancelled. Should have referred her on to Matt. Why hadn't he?

"You haven't heard a word." Lexi raised her voice slightly, forcing his attention back to her. "I'm not sure why you insisted on having coffee if you're not interested in what I have to say." Her cheeks were still flushed, although her erratic breathing had evened out.

He massaged his forehead and thought about her orgasm in the lift. "I'm sorry," he said. "It's not you—"

"Headache?" she asked.

He nodded. "Blinding." Made worse by sexual frustration.

She scratched around in her bag and pulled out a box of painkillers. "Help yourself."

Gratefully, he accepted the box, drinking two pills down with a gulp of coffee. He wondered if somewhere in her bag she had a cure for a massive erection.

"Better?" she asked.

"It will be. Thanks." He passed the box back to her.

"Look, Mr. Riley—"

"Adam," he corrected and repressed a smile. "After what we've shared, 'mister' sounds a little too formal, don't you think?"

"Look...Adam." The color in her face deepened. "Regardless of what...we've shared, or of what just happened, I'm only here to discuss the sibling program. I'm honestly not interested in trading insults or arguing with you. Or making reference to...us. Can you handle that? Can we keep this meeting on a strictly professional basis? To be blunt, the project's too important to me to waste my time with anything else."

This time he couldn't hold back his smile. "Go ahead, Lexi. You have my full attention."

For a moment she just stared at him, then she blinked and shook her head. "As I said, the initial letter I sent outlines the basics of the project. This proposal is more detailed." She pushed a folder to him. "Anything we don't cover today is mentioned in there. The project will be based at POWS, even though it's not aimed at the patients. Its primary purpose is to provide support to siblings of children with cancer."

Adam settled back in his seat. Despite his headache, she had his full attention and he knew she could see it. Her tone warmed to her subject.

"The siblings are the forgotten victims in the fight against cancer. All focus is put on the sick child, which is understandable. The problem is, the brothers and sisters also experience anxiety and distress, and their needs are often overlooked by parents and caregivers in the struggle to treat the patient."

Adam nodded. The trend wasn't foreign to him—he knew more than any person should need to about childhood cancer.

Lexi continued. "These kids have to adapt to so many new things so quickly, the experience can be overwhelming. Their once healthy siblings are sick. How are they supposed to cope? Apart from the obvious worry about the sibling, they may also experience associated guilt, guilt that they're healthy and the sibling's not. Or there's the fear that they could get sick too. They have no control of the situation. They've learned the hard way that no one's invincible."

"It's a traumatic lesson," Adam agreed.

"And there's so much more," Lexi said, her voice filled with passion. "They need to learn new patterns of relating to other family members. All the family dynamics change. For example, parents may focus more on the sick child, neglecting the healthy sibling. Or that sibling may suddenly find him or herself looking after younger siblings, or doing the housework, or performing other roles formerly done by the parents."

She paused and took another sip of coffee. Her eyes settled on his face. "How's your head?"

He nodded, surprised. "A little better, actually."

"Good." She smiled and got straight back to business. "These kids have no outlet for their new emotions and anxieties. Their parents are involved with the sibling. The sibling is often too ill to speak to, and their friends can't comprehend what they're going through. Where do they turn? Whom do they talk to?"

"There are counselors at the hospital, social workers and psychologists like yourself. Surely it's your role to speak to these children."

Lexi nodded. "It is and we do. Most times, however, intervention is aimed at the parents and the sick child. Don't get me wrong, plenty of siblings receive counseling or are referred to appropriate support groups, and they do well. It's the ones who slip through the cracks who suffer. Our project targets all the siblings, not just those lucky enough to have already been reached by the system."

"So what is it exactly you plan to do? Why do you think you

can reach these children when others before you haven't?"

"We intend to identify siblings from the first hospital admission. When a new patient is admitted, notes will be made about siblings, and the information sent through to us. When the time is right, a staff member will approach the parents to discuss the possibility of the siblings joining the program."

"When the time is right?"

"The family's in crisis. They'd need time to adjust to both the illness and the treatment before we introduced the concept of sibling intervention. We can't let too much time pass, though. The siblings are in crisis too, and the sooner we get to them, the better."

"So what will your program offer?"

"It's a threefold service with a primary focus on counseling and support. We'd also offer education about the disease, maybe even a chance for the kids to meet with the doctors and ask questions that their parents can't or won't answer. Finally, the program would give the children a place to go when they don't know where else to turn."

"Where would your offices be?"

"Next to the pediatric oncology ward. I have approval from the hospital board to utilize a few empty rooms. We'd convert them into a lounge, a toy room, a counseling room and an office for the staff members."

"Who is the 'we' you keep referring to?"

"Hospital social workers and nurses who have volunteered to help. I still need a full-time person to coordinate and manage the whole project. Someone new. The volunteers can't give more than a few hours a week of their time. They already have full-time jobs."

"What about you? This is your baby, why not see it

through?" She'd be good for the job. She knew her stuff and she obviously had an invested interest in the program. Most of all, she cared.

Lexi laughed. "I'm already employed full time by the hospital. I'd be able to set a few hours aside each week to help out, but it's not enough to ensure the program runs smoothly."

"Why the interest in this specific program?" He knew the answer. He knew almost everything about her.

Lexi hesitated. She gave him a wary look, then shrugged. "I was once one of those kids. When I was ten, my sister was diagnosed with leukemia."

"Is she...did she survive?"

"Yeah. She's one of the lucky ones."

"What was it like for you, when she was sick?" He shouldn't ask, shouldn't find out any more about her. He couldn't help himself.

"A year straight from hell," Lexi said. "I was too young to grasp the severity of the situation. Sarah was sick, my parents were devastated and the family almost fell apart." She played with her coffee cup. "I was an emotional wreck, swinging from sad to happy, to angry to jealous. I had trouble concentrating at school, and apart from my brother, I didn't have any real support." She looked him dead in the eye. "I could really have used a little professional help then."

"What about now?" Was she over the trauma or did it still haunt her?

"I've worked through it. Took a while, though. I would have coped better if I'd received intervention when Sarah was first diagnosed."

"And thus the sibling program?"

"And thus the sibling program," she agreed. "Far as I'm

concerned, POWS can provide a way more comprehensive and holistic service if we treat the whole family and not just the patient."

Lexi cared, Adam realized. She gave a damn about what happened to people, even if she didn't know them—and she had no trouble showing it.

A sudden sense of claustrophobia overpowered him. He had to get away from her. Once before he'd seen this side of her. At her brother's exhibition. He'd liked that she gave a damn. He'd liked it too much. Now it scared him shitless. What if she began to care about him? What if she began to show it? Worse, what if he began to care about her?

He wouldn't. AJ Riley flew solo. Full stop. She might be the caring type. He wasn't. Not any more.

Damn it, he had to get away.

"Okay. What's the bottom line here? Give me a figure, how much do you need?"

She frowned in confusion and he couldn't blame her. One minute he acted warm and interested, and the next, cold and dismissive.

"Fifty thousand dollars—to start. That's a rough estimate, though. The proposal includes a detailed costs analysis."

He gave the document a cursory glance, then put it on the seat beside him. Later, he'd go over it with a fine-toothed comb, the way he went over any business document. In the meantime, he had more pressing matters to deal with.

"You're good, Lexi, you know that?" He deliberately kept his voice colder than the deadened area in his heart.

"I beg your pardon?"

"Your little show was good. I almost bought the 'I'm innocent' act."

"What?" she spluttered, "you still think I slept with you to get your money?"

"Didn't you?"

Her face turned scarlet.

"It worked," he told her. "Must have been the added extra in the lift earlier. I'm honestly considering giving you the funds." He leered at her breasts, hating himself as he did it. "If you'd consider trying to convince me again."

Lexi flew out of her seat. Grabbing her almost empty cup, she threw the dregs in his face. The cold coffee hit him square in the eyes and dripped down his nose and cheeks.

"Mr. Riley," she bit out, "why don't you take your money and shove it where the sun doesn't shine?" She grabbed her briefcase and marched off. Before she'd taken three strides, she whirled back and glared at him. "If you should mistakenly believe that the sun does shine down there, trust me, you're wrong. And I should know, I've seen it."

Chapter Six

Lexi slammed her purse on her desk and sat. She switched on her computer and tried to take a deep, calming breath. She'd wrongly assumed a good night's sleep would put a little distance between her and her rage. Fifteen hours later, she was every bit as pissed off as she had been yesterday afternoon.

Riley wasn't just a cold, callous bastard. He was a complete prick. She despised him. His drop-dead-gorgeous looks and sexy-as-sin body only made her despise him more.

How dare he make such insinuations? Did the asshole really believe she'd have slept with him if she knew who he was? Professionalism would have stopped her long before it ever got to that point. Besides, she would have been way too busy running the intricate details of her project by him to even consider sex.

Okay—she would have considered it. No way in hell she could look at the man and not think about sex. He was sex personified. Sex oozed from every pore. Even if the meeting in his office had been their first, Lexi would have fantasized her way through the entire appointment. Hardcore fantasies, no doubt. Dammit, she would never have carried through on the thoughts. She was a social worker at the hospital, for God's sake, a professional seeking out his financial assistance. What kind of a woman did he think she was?

Stupid question. She knew exactly what kind of woman he thought she was.

Now where the hell would she find the money? Even if Riley offered it to her, accepting it would make her look like the proverbial whore. How else could she raise the necessary funds? Riley had been her last and best bet.

While she'd waited the six weeks for her appointment to see him, she'd spoken to dozens of other potential backers and pitched her best line to them. All had liked it. Some had been very impressed. A few had even offered to help out with small amounts. None had been able or willing to foot the entire bill. Riley had honestly been her last hope.

Shit.

Her enthusiasm slipped slowly away. If she couldn't get the money from Riley, where would it come from? Fifty thousand dollars wasn't just going to materialize before her eyes. Her shoulder began to twinge annoyingly as she contemplated her options.

Another fundraiser? Daniel's photographic exhibition was just a few months behind them. It wasn't feasible to think of a second huge event so soon. Sure, the general public wanted to help where they could, but their pockets weren't bottomless. Everyone had a cap, and two major fundraisers in under six months was over the top. Even Lexi could see that.

The twinge tightened into a small knot on her shoulder and she kneaded it. There was a very real possibility she might not be able to start up her support program. Would she have to shelve the idea? That was the last thing she'd considered. She couldn't give up on the program. What about all those kids who hadn't been reached? All those kids who wouldn't get support in the future?

The knot replicated itself on her other shoulder.

She considered going back to the hospital board and throwing herself at their mercy. Maybe if she asked *very* nicely, they'd foot the bill.

It wouldn't happen. The hospital was strapped for cash. Whatever extra they had, they siphoned straight into POWS and targeted it at medical treatment. Psychological intervention aimed at healthy siblings, while important, was simply not considered primary medical care. Not when lives where at stake and money was limited.

Hot pinpricks of tension ran up her neck. All her hard work and plans unravelled at her feet. Her project was falling apart and there wasn't a damn thing she could do about it. Where could she get the money?

Her dream had just come to a careening halt. Lexi blinked back tears. Her vision lay in tatters.

Her neck stiffened into a pressure board of tension. She'd have massaged the vicious knots, but by now the simple task of lifting her hands to her neck was too painful.

Shit. Shit, shit, shit. Her plan had failed. The bottom had dropped out.

It had all been so clear. With a little money and the right people, the program would have been brilliant. In her mind's eye she could hear the voices of the kids as they sat together, chatting and laughing. She could feel the hope and the optimism that reverberated through the centre.

For the first time Lexi had failed at something she'd set her mind to. She tapped on the desk. Failure—the word did not sit well with her. She tapped a little faster. All because of AJ "Asshole" Riley. No money. No program. Failure. All because of him.

She had to acknowledge it was all over. The project had just died a quick and unexpected death. All thanks to Riley.

Bullshit.

Where that little voice had come from, Lexi had no idea. Nevertheless, it stopped her musings short. Bullshit?

Yes, damn it. Bullshit. If her plan had failed, it had nothing to do with Riley. Pinning all her hopes on one person was just plain dumb. It wasn't his responsibility to make sure the project worked. It was Lexi's. Why should he care what happened to the siblings? He'd never had a sibling with cancer. It had nothing to do with him. This was her baby. Not his. If she wanted it to work, she had to make it work. Had to come up with another plan. She had to go back to the drawing board and start again.

She'd known all along he might not make the donation. So what if he was the most likely source of money? He wasn't the only source. She could do this. She could make this program work. She'd just have to work harder than she'd ever expected to. A lot harder. The project wasn't going to bum out because AJ bloody Riley thought she was nothing better than a common hooker.

No way. She'd succeed despite the asshole. She'd do it for all those children out there. All the little Daniels and Lexis whose siblings had cancer. Dammit, if she could make it easier for them, she would. She didn't need his help. She could do this without him.

For the kids. It was all for the kids.

Her shoulders relaxed a little and she hit the enter key on her keyboard. She typed feverishly and then hit enter again. The screen blinked and there it was—the file she'd been searching for.

The list of potential donors to POWS.

She'd started the list years before, when she'd first joined the hospital staff. Each year she'd added a couple of names as she learned who the big players in the fundraising game were.

The list had grown substantially. After Daniel's exhibition its numbers were at an all-time high.

She'd find someone on that list to donate money or she'd die trying. No way Riley was stopping her plans. She'd do it without the bastard. She scanned down the screen, waiting for a name to jump out at her, someone she hadn't already contacted. Who would it be?

The Cancer Research Foundation? Their priority was research, not psychosocial support. What about Ronald McDonald House Charity? Nope. They ran their own similar programs. Any money they had, they'd plough back into their own projects. In fact, most of the other foundations on her list worked the same way. They used their cash to fund their own programs.

She considered private companies and scrolled down a couple of pages to the list of buyers from her brother's exhibition. Some of the names were meaningless—she'd never heard of them. Several of them she gave careful consideration and then discarded with a simple shake of her head. Four names sounded familiar and she jotted down their details, considering them viable possibilities.

She'd compiled the list alphabetically, and her pulse quickened as she reached the Rs. Yes, Riley Corporation had been there. They'd bought four photos—and donated them straight back to the hospital, where they now hung at the entry to POWS. With the hefty price tag attached to each picture, the generosity of the company had, by no means, been small.

She drummed the desk and wondered who'd represented Riley's at the exhibition. At the time, she'd been so wrapped up in the success of the evening she hadn't taken note. Could Adam have been there?

Surely not. She would have noticed him. Hell, she would

have sensed his presence across that cavernous gallery, pulling her like a magnet.

Maybe not. She'd hardly had a minute to herself that night. By the time the hive of activity had slowed to a gentle buzz, most of the crowd had left. The only people remaining behind so late into the night had been the core group involved in the exhibition set up, POWS staff members and close family and friends.

If Adam had been there, he'd have left by the time she'd had a chance to notice him. It was immaterial. She didn't have time to ponder the matter. She needed to secure funds for the project.

Half an hour later she rang through to the department secretary.

"Penny, I need your help," she said when the petite blonde appeared in her office. She was on a mission and time was wasting. "This is a list of companies I'm thinking of approaching for money for the sibling program. Can you please do a little more research on them? Find out who the right people are to contact and when would be the best time to contact them. Also, please make up six more files of the proposal and send them off to those people. By the time I phone them, I want them to know who I am and why I'm trying to get in touch with them."

Penny looked confused as she took the sheet of paper from her. "You're still trying to raise funds?"

"Yes," she said, trying to keep the bitterness from her voice. "I'm afraid I had no luck at Riley Corporation yesterday." There was the understatement of the century. "I have to look elsewhere."

"I don't understand..."

"Let's just say, um, AJ Riley and I didn't get off to a great start. He's somewhat less enthralled with the project than I'd hoped."

Penny shook her head, looking no less puzzled for Lexi's explanation. "Well, if that's the case, why did Mr. Riley just phone to say he'd approved your request?"

"What?"

"AJ Riley phoned not five minutes ago. He was in a hurry and didn't speak for long, just told me to tell you that you had the go-ahead. The funds were yours."

Lexi gaped at Penny.

"I was on my way to your office to tell you when you buzzed," the secretary said.

"What the fuck is he up to?" Lexi muttered to herself.

"Pardon?"

"Nothing." Lexi shook her head. "Just thinking out loud."

What the hell kind of a game was Riley playing? He'd made his expectations quite clear. If she wanted the money, she'd have to sleep with him again. She'd told him where to shove his offer, yet he'd gone and approved the donation anyway. Just what exactly did the conniving bastard want in return?

More importantly, would she accept the money? How could she and still look him in the eye? She knew what he thought of her. Far as he was concerned, she'd earned it. A good night's sex for a healthy little donation.

Good work, Tanner.

Now what? Would he expect her to sleep with him again? A small "thank you" for his generous gift? Would she want to sleep with him again? *Bugger.* She hadn't meant to think about that.

The bastard had her in a no-win situation. If she accepted the donation, she looked like a hooker. If she didn't, the program suffered.

The bastard. The cold, callous, heartless, cruel, vindictive bastard.

"He must be a nice man," Penny said thoughtfully.

"Oh, yes." Lexi snorted. "He's a real charmer. Tell me, did he say anything else to you?"

"Just that he'd be in touch and you should wait for his call so you could iron out all the little details."

"I should wait for his call?" Lexi asked, suddenly livid.

"That's what he said."

Lexi grabbed her keys and bag. "Arrogant asshole," she snarled. "How dare he assume I would sit around waiting for his call?"

It was Penny's turn to gape. "Where are you going?"

"I'm going to have a chat with that nice man. If he wants to iron out the little details, believe me, I'm more than willing to press a couple of facts home."

∞

She marched into Genevieve's office, gave her a curt nod and walked straight to Riley's door.

As she reached for the handle, the secretary blurted out, "Miss Tanner, you can't go in there."

Watch me. "Is he in a meeting?"

"No. He asked not to be disturbed."

"Too late. He's already deeply disturbed." She threw the door open, stepped inside and slammed it shut behind her.

He looked up from his work, his face bland, save for a raised eyebrow.

"You and I have a few details to straighten out," she told

him without preamble. God, did he have to look so unbelievably sexy in his designer suit and loosened tie? Did he know that icy look of his got her so hot she could just about combust in his office? What was it about the damn man that made her want to kill him and fuck him all at the same time?

His tone matched his expression. "Well, well, Lexi. Isn't this a surprise?"

Surprise? More like a nasty shock. She hated him, yet all she could think of as she glared at him was how good he'd looked naked.

"Mr. Riley, I'm sorry," a breathless voice said behind her. "I tried to stop her. She just barged straight in."

He gave an almost imperceptible nod. "That's okay, Genevieve. I'll take it from here."

"If you're sure?"

"I am. Thank you," he added dismissively, and the door closed behind her.

"What the hell are you up to, Riley?" she demanded. "What's the deal with the money?"

His eyes mocked her. "I thought you'd be happy to have the funds. Isn't that what you wanted all along?"

"Don't mess with me. You behaved deplorably yesterday. You knew full well I never expected to hear from you again. So just what is it you're trying to achieve?" She marched forward, set her hands on the desk and stared him straight in the eye. "Nobody would insult another person like you did me, and then decide in favor of giving them money. It doesn't make sense." She took a deep breath and narrowed her eyes. "You don't make sense. I can only surmise that you have some hidden agenda in all of this, and I want to know what it is."

Riley smirked. "You make it sound like I'm running some

sort of covert operation."

"I have no idea what kind of operation you're running, I just know I don't like the way you run it. What's the deal, Riley? Why are you giving me the money?"

"Frankly, that is none of your business."

"None of my business?" she spluttered. "It's one hundred percent my business. This project is my baby."

He eyed her in silence for a minute before conceding. "I think it's a good project." A muscle twitched in his cheek. "That's reason enough."

Bull. That wasn't close to reason enough. Riley was hiding something and she knew it. The tone of his voice told her quite clearly that whatever it was, it was deeply personal and, she suspected, really none of her business. Although curiosity nipped at her, she didn't push the issue.

Her program had suddenly found life again, when an hour ago it was almost dead. The teeniest tiniest possibility existed that maybe she would get the sponsorship from Riley Corporation after all. First, she had to clear up any confusion or misconceptions. Lexi had to make it perfectly clear that whatever happened, if she did accept his sponsorship she would not offer sexual favors in return.

"What about the strings?" She almost didn't want to hear the answer.

"Strings?"

Oh, the innocence with which he asked. She could have kicked him. "What strings does this money come attached to? What do you want from me in return?"

He focused his cold eyes on her chest, and against her will her breasts heaved. "I thought I made that clear yesterday."

"Bastard," she hissed. "I won't get into this again. I did not sleep with you for your money and I will not sleep with you in return for money. Period. Thank you for your...offer. I reject it. Cold." She straightened her back in preparation to leave.

He spoke before she could turn around. The low, seductive quality to his tone stopped her from going anywhere.

"You don't like the...strings attached?"

"It's not just the strings I don't like. It's you, too." She fervently wished she could say that and really mean it. As much as she loathed him, her body still responded to his proximity and to his masculine smell and seductive voice. Prickles of awareness ran down her spine and lodged in the small of her back, sending pulses of desire thrumming through her body.

"I think the strings could be rather...fulfilling, don't you?" He sat back in his chair and looked her up and down. His movements were slow and lazy and captivated her with their leisure. "Perhaps I can make the offer a little more enticing?" He stared at her from beneath a thick fringe of black lashes. His eyes were fiery rocks of blue ice, desire blazing in them.

The look on his face paralyzed her. She couldn't move, couldn't draw breath.

"Something happened when you barged into my office." He lowered his voice. "I got an erection, Lexi. I still have it. I'm aroused...very aroused."

Her jaw dropped. Of all the things she'd expected him to say, this was not one of them. His words weaved their magic through her senses, magnifying her awareness of him. His voice rippled like velvet over her skin, and her mouth filled with the taste of his salty flesh. His scent surrounded her, mixing with the remembered smell of their lovemaking—musk and man.

She shivered. Damn it, she didn't want to respond to him, didn't want to want him like she did.

"You hate the thought of it, don't you?" God, his voice. It

83

was so rich and so deep she could almost burrow into it. "The thing is, you're aroused too. I can see it." He lowered his eyes to her chest, and her breasts burned beneath his blistering gaze. "Your nipples are tight, like little pebbles, pushing against your bra. Just like in Melbourne." He took a deep breath. "How would you react if I kissed them now? Placed my mouth over the turgid tips and sucked on them?" He looked into her eyes. "Would you like that?"

Like that? Hell, the very thought of it had her liquefying in his office. Her mouth still hung open, making speech difficult.

"I would," he continued. He laid his palm flat against the middle of his desk. "Almost as much as I'd like to bend you forward over my desk, bunch your skirt high above your hips and slide your thong down your legs." He paused and looked below her waist. Her skirt might as well have been invisible. He stared straight through it at her panties. "You are wearing a thong, aren't you, Lexi? Is it black? I think it is. Black and lacy."

Actually, it was deep purple, and much as she wished it wasn't, it was very, very wet.

"We'd be standing there, where you are now, so you can look out the window while I inch the lace down your legs." Involuntarily, her eyes left his face and flashed to the window. Once again, the breathtaking panorama astounded her. Not quite as breathtaking, though, as the man in front of her, sitting by his desk idly undressing her with his eyes and seducing her with his words.

"I'd move slowly, of course, so I wouldn't miss one centimeter of your silky skin." He looked contemplative for a minute. "Would I take them off with my hands, or my teeth? I can't quite decide."

Tingles ran up her legs as if his teeth grazed her outer

thigh.

He shook his head. "My hands, I think. That way I can see the view. Not the same view you'd be watching, obviously. I'd be staring at your naked ass. I'd be watching as you shove it backwards, and upwards, and tease me with a glimpse of your feminine core." The timbre of his voice changed, lowered a notch. "It's wet, Lexi, isn't it? It always is when you're around me."

Her breath caught in her throat. She had trouble focusing. All she could see, really, was her naked butt in the air and him staring at it, hunger etched in his eyes.

Hell, yes, she was wet. He was right—she always was when she was around him.

"I'll spend a long time just staring at you, watching you gleam in the sunshine. Watching the cream ooze out as you wait for me to touch you."

He licked his lip and she realized she was gnawing on her bottom lip in the exact place where his tongue touched his mouth. The realization was erotic in the extreme. She let her lip slip away from her teeth as she studied his mouth and could almost feel the warm moisture of his tongue on her own lip.

He focused on her mouth, his breath uneven. "I will touch you," he promised. "Just not with my fingers." He clenched his hand into a fist. "Even though they're itching to massage that cream all over your lips. Even though I'm dying to rub your pretty little clit until you writhe beneath the contact." He paused. "I won't use my fingers, because you don't want them."

Oh, dear Lord, was he ever wrong. She wanted them so bad she could imagine them between her legs.

"I won't use my tongue either," he said, and again he licked his lower lip. "Much as I'd like to taste all that sweet honey on offer, to lick away every last drop, I won't do that, because it's not my tongue you want."

Oh. Yes. It. Is. The thought of him kneeling beneath her, between her legs, with his face lifted upward and his mouth kissing her intimately, made her tremble uncontrollably.

"No." He shook his head. "Not my tongue. See, I'll use my cock. It's hard and it's ready and it's what you need. It's what you want. I'll push your back down, gently, until your breasts are squashed against the cold, smooth wood of this desk." He relaxed his hand, ran it over the wood in much the same way she wished he'd run it over her lower back. "Then I'll pull your hips back so that you're high, and you're open, and you're ready for me. And then," he paused and closed his eyes for a minute, as if in pain. "And then," he said in a hoarse voice, "I'll fuck you. I'll shove my cock so deep inside you, you'll scream for more. I'll shove every last inch in so deep you'll think we were one person." His voice caught and he opened his eyes. "And I'll do it over and over again until you think you can't take it for one...more...second. At which point..." he stopped, stared straight into her soul and said, "I'm going to make you come. It'll be the sweetest, most powerful orgasm you'll ever have and you'll be glad you're lying on the desk, because if you weren't, the strength of your climax would knock you off your feet."

She knew he was right. No way she'd be physically capable of taking all that pleasure standing up. Her knees would give in the second he plunged into her.

"While you're coming, while you're so high on the sexual gratification only I can give you, I'll come too." He closed his eyes again, as if the effort involved in keeping them open was just too great. "The way you shudder when you come, and the way you clench around my cock... Christ, I'll have no choice," he whispered. "You'll milk me of every last drop. Leave me depleted and exhausted and fully, fully satisfied." He took a deep breath. "We'll both be fully satisfied." His eyes opened.

"Afterwards, I'll collapse on top of you. Then, for a very long time, neither of us will have the energy, or the will, to move."

Neither of them spoke. They simply remained as they were, she standing, he sitting, and stared at each other. The only sound was that of uneven, raspy breathing—his and hers.

An interminable length of time passed before Lexi broke the silence. "I... Well... Right then." Because after that, what else could she have said?

It must have had an effect on Adam, because he snapped out of his trancelike state. He rested his elbow on the edge of the desk and dropped his forehead into his hand. "Christ, Lexi, I'm sorry." His voice was rough. There was no mistaking the sincerity in it. He shook his head. "I never meant for that to happen."

Lexi gawked at him.

After another moment, he raised his head and looked at her. Both the icy glare and the hungry stare were gone. He just looked tired. "I was way out of line and I apologize." He shook his head again, as though unable to believe what he'd just done. She could barely believe it herself.

Then he shrugged and straightened his tie. "The donation comes with no attached strings. I...Riley Corporation would be happy to give you the money. I spent a long time reviewing your proposal last night and I believe your project is both necessary and useful. I think it would benefit any child who took part in it. It's that simple."

The man changed personas faster than she changed outfits on a bad clothes day. He perplexed her.

"I'm not sure what to say," she told him. She wasn't even sure what to think. His verbal seduction left her body humming crazily from overstimulation and lack of fulfillment. His change in attitude stunned her. Was she supposed to be the professional social worker all over again, here to make a formal acceptance of a donation for her POWS program? Or was she supposed to be the spurned, insulted lover who, for the third time, had fallen for the evil, sexy charmer who treated her like dirt?

At this point, the only thing she was capable of being was enormously aroused and virtually speechless.

"There's nothing to say," he answered. "My partner, the financial director of Riley Corporation, Matt Brodie, will be in touch with you to discuss the transfer of funds. You can tell him whether you'd prefer it in a lump sum or in monthly deposits. In addition, we'll need to handle the press. As soon as they get wind that we've made another donation to the hospital, they'll be sniffing around for details. Matt will liaise with our PR department about that. I will expect monthly reports on the progress of the program and detailed analyses of where the funds have been used. I can get that from Matt." He paused and made a note of something in his diary. Then he looked her square in the eyes. "Any questions you have, Matt will be happy to deal with. Genevieve will give you his card on your way out."

"You won't be involved in the process from now on?" Lexi asked.

"No. I've done my share. The rest can be handled by Brodie and his staff."

She could scarcely believe what happened. On the one hand, everything fell into place. She had the funds, she could start the program and she could watch her idea come to fruition. On the other hand, he'd just cut her out of his life and passed her on to someone else so he wouldn't have to deal with her anymore. From now on, there would be no reason to meet Adam Riley again.

Why wasn't she filled with elation?

"Well, then." She smiled nervously. "I suppose all that remains to be expressed is our gratitude." She tried to slip back into social work mode. "On behalf of POWS and the hospital, I thank you for your donation toward the sibling program. Please rest assured the money will be put to good use and many children will benefit from your generosity."

He gave a brief nod. "You're welcome."

Lexi had spent several awkward moments in Adam's company. This had to be the most uncomfortable one yet. She didn't want to thank him and leave. She wanted him to press her down over the desk and fuck her thoroughly, just like he'd described. Sure, she didn't want it in exchange for the money, but she wanted Adam. Wanted him with a ferocity that stunned her.

"So I guess this is it." She gave him a half-smile.

"I guess it is." He nodded in agreement.

"I should probably be going then."

"You probably should."

Well then, why were her legs not moving? "Goodbye, Mr. Riley."

"Goodbye, Miss Tanner."

She bit her lip, wanting to say something more but not sure what. Finally, she sighed, walked to the door and opened it.

She turned back to him. "Adam..." Her voice caught and trailed off as she saw his face. It looked haunted, overshadowed by a profound sadness the likes of which she hadn't seen before—and working at POWS, she'd been witness to many sorrowful expressions.

She lost her track of thought.

"Yes, Lexi?" he prompted, his voice soft.

Somehow, she knew that was the last time she'd hear him

call her name. "You..." What could she say? She couldn't intrude on his thoughts. "I..." In the end, the only thing that came to mind was a simple, "Thank you, Adam."

The last thing she saw of him was a single, responsive nod of his head.

Chapter Seven

"Doesn't anybody knock anymore?" Adam muttered as, five minutes after Lexi left, the door to his office opened yet again and Matt Brodie sauntered inside. Routine was routine. Why should it change now? Matt never knocked. He merely walked in and made himself comfortable—usually stopping at the glass cabinet to fix a drink first.

Adam checked his watch. Even by Matt's standards, it was too early for a scotch. Damn pity. He could use one himself. A double, straight up. He hadn't meant to pitch that seduction line at Lexi. God help him, she'd stood there, a silhouette in the sunlight, her hair a halo of gold behind her, and he'd only been able to think about making love to her. He would have given his left arm to press her down on his desk and fuck her from behind, to plunge his dick into her repeatedly until she convulsed around him.

"Word is you've made another hefty donation to the hospital," Matt said as he took a seat, stretched his legs out and rested his hands on his stomach.

"Word gets around quickly," Adam answered noncommittally. His tone was a notch lower than he would have liked it and he cleared his throat.

"So it's true?"

Adam nodded, not quite trusting his voice yet.

"Don't you think you've given enough?"

"Don't you think it's none of your business?" Okay, that sounded more normal. Long as he didn't think of her naked ass, he'd be just fine.

"Hmm, let's see. Financial director...five-figure donation...Riley Corporation?" Matt scratched his chin. "Well, gosh and doggone it, I do believe it could be my business after all."

Adam smirked, focusing on the man he viewed as a brother. "Yeah, yeah. Whatever."

"You want to tell me what's going on? I thought we'd discussed this and decided not to donate any more to this particular cause." His voice held no edge, just concern.

"No," Adam answered, "we discussed it and you decided. I didn't come to any kind of conclusion."

"You're too close to this one and you know it. You have no objectivity when it comes to dealing with this shit. The request should never have been handled by you, it should have been referred on to me."

"Relax," he placated, "it has been. Miss Tanner will be dealing directly with you from now on."

Matt was not placated. "Why'd you take it on yourself to meet with the woman in the first place?"

Adam smiled ruefully. God knows he never should have met with Lexi, but some forces even an adult man couldn't fight. "She made the appointment with Genevieve while I was away. I didn't know what she wanted until the day of the meeting."

Matt shook his head and stood. "It screws you up. Every time." He opened the bar, and to Adam's immense relief, pulled out a bottle of whiskey and two glasses. "Here," he said, placing a glass in front of Adam and half filling it with the tawny liquid. "Single malt, no ice. Yeah. It is a healthy serving. You look like you could use it."

Yup. He sure could, and he did, bolting back a large mouthful. The scotch burned its way down his throat and settled in a warm puddle in his stomach.

Matt raised an eyebrow, poured himself a tot and sat back down. "So, what charity is it?"

"Siblings of kids with cancer."

"Siblings?" Matt snorted. "You mean the healthy kids who get to live normal lives?"

"Nope, I mean the healthy kids whose normal lives get buggered up by cancer."

Matt nodded and swirled his glass. "Point taken," he acquiesced. "Tell me about it."

He set his drink down. "It's a good project, Matt. She's looking at cancer from a whole different angle, one we'd...I'd never considered before." He gave his partner a brief synopsis of the program. "She'll do good things with the money. This wasn't a mistake."

"Got any information on it?"

Adam opened a drawer and handed him the proposal. "It's all in there. Anything else you want to know, contact Lexi Tanner. Her details are on the cover sheet."

Matt took a couple of minutes to browse through the document. Then he nodded. "It does look good. I still don't think you should've gotten personally involved."

Adam held back a cynical laugh. If Matt knew just how involved he'd gotten, he'd fall off his chair. "Listen, mate, quit worrying about this. It's the right decision."

"For the hospital maybe. Not for you."

Adam rubbed a tired hand over his face. Was it really still morning? Seemed more like midnight.

"You know I'm right, Adam. The only time you get that look on your face is when you think about Timmy."

For a moment neither man spoke. Matt's words hung in the air between them. Tension crackled up Adam's spine and he threw back the rest of his drink. He barely tasted it. Pain cut through him, raw and unforgiving. It *was* about Timmy. It was always about Timmy.

Adam shook his head. "I think about him all the time."

Matt nodded. "I know you do, mate." His gentle tone only served to increase Adam's pain. "Look, no worries. I'll take care of the project from here on." He gave him a no-nonsense glare. "You just stay out of it. Understood?"

"Don't you have some work to do? Or some clients to harass?"

"Apparently, I have a whole new charity proposition to deal with."

"Good, then why don't you go take care of it and leave me in peace?"

Matt stood. "My leaving," he said, his voice forceful yet compassionate, "is not going to give you peace. Only you can find that—when you're ready to start looking."

Chapter Eight

Friday afternoon found Lexi staring across her desk at Matt Brodie. They'd been together for about an hour and had managed to sort out most of the details pertaining to the Riley donation.

Over a week had passed since she'd seen Adam, and maybe forty-five seconds since she'd thought about him. The man occupied every inch of her head. Confusion about him etched its way through her heart. One minute she despised him and everything he stood for, the next she hungered for a glimpse of him. More than once she'd thought about the expression on his face when she'd turned from the door in his office to look at him.

She didn't need the details to know Adam was hiding something utterly devastating, something traumatizing. Her instinctive reaction had been to soothe the hurt but Riley had made it clear he wanted nothing to do with her. Offering him comfort would probably only have compounded the animosity of their already stormy relationship.

Dealing with Matt was a breeze compared to her interactions with Riley. Matt seemed like a decent man. He was good looking in a wholesome kind of a way with brown hair, brown eyes covered by slim, wire-framed glasses, and a quick smile that put her instantly at ease. Perhaps her comfort with him was compounded by the fact that he lacked the brute sexuality his partner exuded.

His no-nonsense manner made their business interactions a pleasure. In less than an hour, they'd decided that the donation would be made on a monthly basis for a year. Thereafter they would assess the viability of the project and renegotiate funding. If the project was successful, Riley Corporation would continue to provide the necessary capital.

Lexi had given him a tour of the ward and the adjoining rooms that would be used for the project and introduced him to the staff members who would be participating in the program. They'd discussed a suitable salary for the soon-to-be appointed manager and identified a feasible commencement date. Now they sat ironing out the last few fine points of their contract.

Lexi glanced at the notes she'd jotted down before Matt arrived. "The last matter on the agenda—keeping you informed of proceedings. Adam has requested that we send monthly rep—" Matt's eyes widened in astonishment. "Is something wrong?"

"What did you just say?"

"I was talking about sending you monthly reports."

"No, before that. Who did you say requested them?"

"Mr. Riley. Why?"

"You called him Adam."

"Yes?"

"You called AJ Riley Adam."

Lexi lifted her eyebrows in question.

Matt took off his glasses and grinned. "No one calls him Adam. I didn't think anyone in Sydney even knew his first name."

So. It was out of character for Riley to introduce himself as

Adam? She tucked that little piece of information away to ponder over another time. "Would it make you more comfortable if I called him AJ? Or Mr. Riley?"

"Not at all," Matt assured her, a strange gleam to his eyes. "I'm sorry, I've gone off track." He put his glasses back on. "What were you saying about monthly reports?"

"Just that...Adam has requested we keep you up-to-date with them. I'd also like to invite you over from time to time to see the progress we're making. If the children are up to it, possibly even have you meet some of them."

"That sounds fine," he said. "I'd quite like that. Once you're officially up and running and the rooms are ready, we'll be sending a photographer around to document the project. There'll be a lot of public interest in this."

"Perhaps on the opening day we can hold a small press conference? That will cover any media needs for both Riley Corporation and the hospital, and it will give the project some much-needed publicity. The more parents out there who are aware of it, the better. Once the program begins, I won't allow press or photographers into the offices. I won't subject our kids to that."

Matt nodded. "I wouldn't expect you to." He looked down at his own notes. "Any other issues to discuss?"

"None," Lexi said. "How about you?"

"Nothing right now. If you think of anything, feel free to contact me at any time."

"Thank you, and same here." Lexi checked her watch. "Now if you don't mind, I'm going to have to call an end to this meeting. I have a pressing matter that needs my attention."

"Hospital work. I understand."

"Good guess, but nope." Lexi smiled. "This one's much

closer to home. My brother's getting married on Sunday and it's time for me to spend some quality sibling time with him."

∞

Lexi looked at Daniel and sighed in envy. Her brother had a permanent grin plastered on his face. He'd had it since Amy'd agreed to marry him. He'd also spent an inordinate amount of time hugging Lexi just because she was his sister. Sarah had left the room minutes earlier to escape being crushed in yet another brotherly embrace.

"Can you believe it?" he asked with one of his stupid smiles. "In less than an hour, I'll be a married man."

It was pretty hard to believe. Daniel'd always been a diehard bachelor, a non-believer in the whole commitment story. Today was his wedding day. Who'd ever have thought? Daniel Tanner—a groom. No question about it, he was a changed man. There was a sense of completion about him that hadn't been there before his best friend accepted his proposal.

Lexi envied him. She wanted what he had—a lifelong commitment with the person he loved. Daniel's life was full. Hers was not. No matter how busy or exciting her days were, her nights always stretched out long and empty, with no one to come home to at the end of the day. No one to talk to, to snuggle up to, to make love to. No one. Just her.

For a few hours with Adam, before she'd discovered his identity, she'd experienced a brief sense of the wholeness that Daniel now displayed. It wasn't enough. It was gone before she'd even sniffed at it, and she wanted it back. Not with Riley, obviously. With someone who could still the loneliness in her. Someone who could fill up that emptiness.

"I bet she outdazzles the sun," Daniel gushed.

Lexi stuck her finger in her mouth and made gagging noises. "God, you're pathetic. If I'd known you'd behave like this, I'd never have helped you in your plans to get Amy."

For about the millionth time that day, Daniel picked her up and twirled her around. "Did I ever thank you for your help? I couldn't have done it alone, you know." Did he ever thank her? More like, did he ever stop thanking her?

"Oh please," Lexi brushed him off, "I've seen the way Amy looks at you now. You could have sent her a text message telling her you love her and she would have fallen for you."

He grinned again. "Yeah, still. A bit of gentle nudging was a lot more effective. Who knows, Lex, maybe one day I can return the favor."

Lexi's smile faded. "Yeah, who knows? Maybe one day you can." If Daniel could find a woman he wanted to make a lifelong commitment to, surely there was someone out there for her? Her mind flashed on Riley's sculpted chest. Someone who didn't make her feel like a common call girl every time he saw her.

Lexi stood with her mother and sister as the newlyweds posed for photographs.

"I can't believe Daniel didn't insist on taking the pictures himself," Lexi whispered in wonder.

"I can't believe he can take his eyes off Amy long enough to look at a camera, never mind take a picture." Sarah chuckled.

"It wasn't so long ago that you were the one who couldn't drag your eyes off Steven," Molly, their mother, said with affection, and they all turned to watch Sarah's husband in his desperate attempt to catch their four-year-old son, Benjamin, before he knocked yet another glass off the pristine tables in the reception hall.

The guests trickled in, and Daniel and Amy smiled for the last few shots before turning to greet everyone. The band played softly in the background and waiters walked around with platters of canapés and other tasty morsels to tide the crowds over until dinner.

Lexi accepted the congratulations and kisses of ten thousand well-wishers before finally taking her seat at her table along with Sarah and her family. After Daniel and Amy danced the first dance, other family members and guests rose to join them on the floor.

Lexi grabbed her nephew's hand. "Come on, Benny. It's time to dance."

"I don't know how," he told her, in all his four-year-old's innocence.

"It's easy, I'll show you. Just stand on my feet and I'll lead you around."

Ben stared at her feet with mistrust. "I don't know, Lekth," he said. "Thothe shoeth look vewy high."

She laughed. Her heels were a little higher than usual but they looked good and that was what mattered. "Don't worry, just hold tight and I promise you won't fall."

In minutes, she was laughing with her nephew as they tried a series of dance steps, looking for a suitable one for a woman of nearly six-feet and a boy who barely reached her hips. Finally, she surrendered to the inevitable and picked Ben up, hugging him tight while she swayed them from side to side.

As Daniel and Amy joined them, Ben tugged at her arm and lisped, "Lex, why is that man staring at you?"

"What man, sweetheart?" Three pairs of eyes turned to look in the direction Ben pointed.

Her stomach lurched as she found the man. His gaze froze her movements, and her heart pounded in her chest. What was he doing here? He looked yummy enough to eat, dressed in a tux and crisp white shirt that showed off his tanned skin and contrasted sharply with his black hair. Lexi swore to herself. Dammit, what happened to the air whenever he was around?

"It's AJ," Daniel said.

"You know him?" Lexi asked, astounded.

"Yep. He came to the exhibition, bought a few of the photos. We've become quite good friends since. We run together about three times a week."

"He's hot," Amy observed, "in a cold kind of a way." She placed a placating hand on Daniel's arm. "Don't panic, Tanner. He doesn't hold a candle to you."

"He'd better not," Daniel huffed and Lexi moved discreetly out of their way as her brother dipped his head toward Amy's.

"Who ith he?" Ben asked, unaware of the acute discomfort the man stirred in her.

"Just a man." A man who threw her world off centre. A man who made her feel as glorious as the rising sun and smaller than the tiniest flea. A man who seemed to turn up every time she came to terms with not seeing him again.

"Well, why's he staring at you?" Ben lisped.

Why was he staring? He'd made it clear he wanted nothing more to do with her by dismissing her from his life and sending Matt to deal with her instead.

"I'm not sure," she told Ben. "Maybe he's wondering who this cute guy is I'm holding."

"No," Ben disagreed. "He's looking at you. Do you know him?"

"Yes, sweetie, I met him through work."

"Then why don't you say hello to him?"

Because that's probably the last thing he wants. Besides, I can't seem to breathe properly when he's around.

"I'll do it if you're too scared," Ben offered and lifted his arm and waved at Riley. "Hello, man," he yelled across the room and Lexi snorted, though in amusement or horror she wasn't certain.

He hadn't taken his eyes off her for a second, not from the minute she'd preceded the bride down the aisle. He'd hidden in the crowds and watched her, content to keep his distance yet drink his fill. Touching her may be off limits but he couldn't stop himself from staring.

She looked stunning. Her dress was the same color as a predawn sky, with a simple line that clung in all the right places. The long slit up the side allowed for an enticing view of shapely thigh—thigh that had been wrapped around his waist, and his neck, more than once in Melbourne. A low neckline showed off slim shoulders and a teasing glimpse of firm, round breasts. Breasts he wanted to bury his face in. Breasts he *had* buried his face in.

He headed over to her, watching as the boy wriggled out of her arms and skipped off to play with another child across the room. He sighed in relief. One less stress to deal with. Dealing with Lexi on her own was hard enough.

She frowned as the child raced away, then she stood a little straighter and flicked her hair over her shoulders as if bracing for his arrival.

"Lexi," he greeted her, keeping his voice neutral.

"Adam." She eyed him nervously.

Who could blame her? Last time she'd seen him he'd said some pretty outrageous things. "Congratulations."

"Thank you."

"They make a handsome couple."

A brief smile touched her mouth as she looked at the bride and groom. "Yes, they do." She turned back to him. "I didn't expect to see you here."

"That would explain the stunned expression on your face."

"I never knew you and Daniel were friends."

"There seems to be quite a few things you never knew about me."

A hint of color touched her cheeks. "Yeah, well that's the thing about meeting someone for the first time. You generally don't know very much about them."

"Does it make you uncomfortable? Knowing you've slept with a friend of your brother's?" Shit, why'd he have to talk about sex every time he saw her? What made him so damn horny all he could think about was hauling her off into some secluded corner and fucking her stupid?

Her eyes blazed. "Not as uncomfortable as it does knowing the friend thinks I slept with him under false pretenses."

"Did you?" The way she got all worked up and hot under the collar like that, well it got him all worked up and hot under the collar.

Her hand fisted at her side and for a minute he thought she might punch him.

"I have answered that question," she bit out and stepped closer, speaking into his ear, her voice soft enough so only he could hear and aggressive enough to get those hot bits under his collar really burning. "Several times. Now, you listen up, and you listen good. This is my brother's wedding and I will not engage in some two-bit discussion with you about what kind of a whore you think I am. I won't do it now, and I won't do it tomorrow or the next day. If you have anything else you need to say to me, I'm sure Matt will be happy to pass on the message. Now, if you'll excuse me, I see someone I would like to spend time with."

Ouch.

As she twisted around to leave, he grabbed her wrist and spun her back to face him.

"Just what the hell do you think you're doing?" she asked in a ferocious whisper. Her smile was tight and her gaze darted around as she checked to see if anyone had noticed their little altercation.

"I'm clearing something up." He kept his voice low.

"I told you, speak to Matt." She tried to pull away. He gave her arm another tug and she teetered on her heels for half a second before losing her balance and stumbling into him. He wrapped his arm around her waist, steadying her and pulling her close at the same time.

"This isn't really something you'd want Matt to hear." Damn, she felt good in his arms.

"Adam, let me g—"

"I don't think you're a whore," he cut her off. "I never did." His mouth was by her ear and his voice was soft. He couldn't help but notice the goosebumps that skittered over her bare shoulder and down her arm.

She stopped struggling. "Then why do you insist on treating me like one?"

Because if I treat you like you ought to be treated, if I give you half a chance, I'll fall for you. "I'm sorry. You don't deserve it. You never have." How could he tell her she scared the crap out of him? How could he explain the only way he knew to keep his distance was to punish her emotionally? She wouldn't understand why he needed to keep his distance, why it hurt too damn much to ever love again.

The fight drained out of her. Her resistance slipped away. "No," she agreed, "I really don't deserve it."

Suddenly, he didn't want to let her go. He wanted to keep on holding her. "Dance with me?"

Her body tensed up again.

"We're on the dance floor anyway and people are beginning to stare." Shit, why'd he need to make excuses to hold her? "It's just a dance, that's all."

She nodded uncertainly and her arms fluttered midair for a minute before she wound them round his shoulders. Shivers ran down his spine as she touched his hair.

For a few minutes, they danced in silence, the music slow and romantic. Her soft curves and firm breasts fit snug against his more solid form. Hard as Adam tried not to, he found himself relaxing into the beat, relaxing against her body.

"Why didn't you tell me you knew Daniel?"

"You never asked." He declined to point out that he'd never told her he knew her, either.

"You might have mentioned you'd be here tonight."

He probably should have said something. "When would you have liked me to tell you? After you threw the coffee at me, or while you were lambasting me about the donation?"

She stiffened in his arms. "This was a bad idea. Thank you for the dance."

"Lexi, wait, I'm sorry. That was supposed to be a joke." He shook his head. "I guess you and I just aren't at a point where we can laugh at ourselves."

She studied his face for a minute. "No, I guess we're not."

"How about we call a truce? Start over fresh. What do you say?"

She gnawed on her lower lip and he thought he might bust a gut watching her.

"I say, I think I'd like that."

"I think I'd like that too."

She looked almost as surprised by his answer as he was. "So we're okay?"

He nodded. "We're okay."

They began to dance again.

"You look exquisite tonight." He was thrown by the sound of his own voice—soft as a lover's whisper.

"Uh, thank you. You look pretty good yourself." She pulled a sheepish face. "I'm sorry. I shouldn't have thrown the coffee at you." Then she gave him an impish grin, a smile that made her dimples stand out and his heart stand still. "It was too cold to have much effect anyway."

He chuckled and she stared at him in delight. "You can laugh."

"I've been known to once in a while," he replied, still smiling. "Don't let that become general knowledge or everyone will expect it." He enjoyed the laughter. It wasn't something he did very often.

"You have a beautiful smile," she told him, her eyes fixed on his mouth.

"Good grief, Miss Tanner." He stopped suddenly. "Do you know you've complimented me twice tonight?"

She grinned. "Don't get used to it, Riley. You have to work hard to earn my compliments."

"Adam," he corrected automatically. "I'm learning that most things about you require hard work." He changed the subject before she could retort. "Cute kid. Who is he?" At least the question came out sounding casual. Asking was torture.

"Ben? My nephew, Sarah's son. He is a cutie. With the tact of an ox, as you might have noticed. We never know what he's going to come out with next."

She was swaying seductively, her body warm and inviting and just a little too right in his arms. "I saw you talking to Sarah earlier. You seem close."

"We are." Lexi nodded toward Daniel. "All three of us are close. What about you? Do you have any brothers or sisters?"

He shrugged. "Not really."

"Not really." She laughed. "What's that supposed to mean? Either you have siblings or you don't."

"Well, technically speaking, I don't. But for a long time I've considered Matt a brother." More information than he needed to give her, perhaps, but something about Lexi made him want to talk.

"He's not just a colleague?"

"I've known him for years. We were at school together. He founded Riley Corporation with me."

"Sounds like a good friend."

"The best. I couldn't have got through..." Adam caught himself just in time. *Jesus, too close.* Images of Timmy flashed before his eyes. It took a couple of seconds to compose his thoughts. "Let's just say we've been there for each other through the years. He helped me through a real rough patch a while back."

Ah, crap. The look on her face told him she'd picked up too much. Her mouth creased in concern, and confused sympathy shadowed her eyes—much the same way it had in his office. He hadn't meant for her to catch him off-guard then. She'd been leaving; she wasn't supposed to turn around.

To her credit, she didn't push the issue. "Matt was a little surprised when I called you Adam."

"Oh, shit." He squeezed his eyes shut. "I'm never going to hear the end of that one." Until a week ago, Matt was the only person in Sydney who knew him as Adam. Since he'd arrived here ten years ago, he'd felt more comfortable with the nickname AJ. It helped keep people at bay—if they didn't know his first name, they couldn't get too personal.

"Am I missing something?" Lexi asked. "Is your real name a secret?"

"Not at all," Adam said. "I usually prefer the name AJ, that's all. No. No more questions. Let's just enjoy the music, shall we?" He pulled her closer.

She wore very high heels, and the added height made dancing cheek to cheek all too easy. Moving like this, with her in his arms, well it was rather nice. Altogether too nice.

He'd surprised himself tonight, showing her a side of himself he rarely let anyone see. He'd made it a firm policy never to allow anyone close again. Lexi was pushing hard on his resolve. Sleeping with her, though necessary, had been a mistake. Sex as a physical release was one thing. Sex as an expression of emotion was another altogether. With Lexi, the boundaries between the two blurred. The more time he spent with her, the more he liked her. The more he liked her, the more he desired her. The more he desired her, the more of a threat she became. As much as he wanted to, there was no way he could sleep with her again and limit the act to sex. He'd feel something, and that would be the biggest threat of all.

Safer to keep her at arm's length.

Unfortunately, he found it difficult to keep his distance from her. Each time he tried, she found some way of breaking down his barriers and getting in anyway.

Like now. She looked at him and smiled, and then snuggled into him and let the music carry them away.

Though his head resisted, his body embraced her. She fit into his arms perfectly. Her breasts were squashed against his chest and her hand played at the nape of his neck. He breathed in her scent. Fresh green leaves mingled with warm wood and a suggestion of something very feminine. She smelled fresh and sexy and carnal and captivating, and not for the first time that night, his body stirred. Shifting slightly, he nestled against her hips, and she pulled her head back and stared into his eyes.

"Adam?" she whispered.

He held her tighter and murmured, "Shh."

For once, instead of arguing with him, she shut up and they danced.

Chapter Nine

"I had an interesting talk with Lexi Tanner the other day." Matt tucked his briefcase under the seat in front of him and fastened his seat belt.

"You did?" Adam feigned disinterest and turned a page of the Sydney Morning Herald.

"Yep. I told you we were meeting to sort out the fundamentals of the donation."

"I assume there were no problems?" He shook his head at a flight attendant, refusing a drink she offered.

"None at all. Quite the contrary. Apart from being intelligent, easy to talk to and most entertaining, Lexi turned out to be quite the babe. I considered asking her out."

At this, Adam looked up sharply. "Did you?"

Matt shook his head and Adam could have sworn his friend smothered a grin. "No. I would have if she hadn't been in such a hurry. Wanted to go and spend some time with her brother, Daniel."

"Good morning, ladies and gentleman, and thank you for flying Qantas, flight QF 411 to Melbourne."

Adam returned his attention to the paper.

Matt leaned in a little closer and spoke over the voice on the intercom. "You never told me she was Tanner's sister."

"Never thought about it," Adam lied.

"Our flying time today will be approximately one hour and thirty minutes," the disembodied voice announced.

"How was the wedding?"

"Good."

"That all?"

"It was a nice wedding."

"Doesn't say very much."

"The bride looked radiant and the groom smiled a lot. It was a happy day."

Matt smirked. "You take a date?"

"Nope. Went alone."

"If you'll direct your attention to the front of the aircraft, our flight attendants will…"

"What about that Roberts woman? I thought you'd take her."

Adam shrugged. "She's history. Got a little too intense for my liking."

"What about Lexi Tanner?"

"What about her?"

"You spend some time together at the wedding?"

"We spoke."

"I'm sure you did."

"Okay, mate, what's your point?" Might as well stop beating round the bush. Matt had something to say—as always—and he wouldn't rest until he'd said it.

"There aren't many people I know around here who refer to you as Adam."

It had to come back to bite him. "Your point being?"

"Point?" Matt shook his head. "No, my man, there's more than one point here."

The plane reversed from its parked position and taxied down the runway.

"Let's do a quick inventory. First—" Matt held up a thumb, "—you meet with a woman you should never have met with. Second—" index finger, "—she talks you into a donation, which you agree to without running it past me or any other board member. Third—" middle finger, "—it turns out the woman's a looker and she calls you Adam." He lifted his ring finger. "Next, you go to her brother's wedding without a date." Then he grinned again and dealt his trump card. "The fifth and most noticeable point of all is that you almost beat the crap out of me when I mentioned I might ask her out."

The plane shot down the runway and lifted off, the pressure forcing Adam back in his seat. Why had he thought for one second he could hide his feelings from Matt? Then again, what was he hiding? The fact that he'd slept with Lexi? That was none of Matt's business. The fact that Lexi was getting under his skin, regardless that he didn't want her there? Not Matt's business, either, but he seemed to be picking up on it anyway.

"So," Matt continued, "in summary, I guess my point is— what is going on with you and Lexi Tanner?"

Damned if he knew the answer himself.

"Mate," Matt said, "I haven't seen you this wound up about a woman in over ten years. What's the deal?"

"Nothing." Maybe if he said it out loud, he'd believe it.

"Yeah, right." Matt disregarded the answer with a dismissive flick of his hand. "You're falling for her, aren't you?"

"No. I am not," Adam denied vehemently.

"Then you won't mind if I ask her out?" Matt smirked

again.

Try it and I will kill you. "Not at all. Go ahead." Adam buried his face in the newspaper, knowing his eyes had narrowed to dangerous slits.

"I'll take her for dinner. Or on a romantic harbor cruise. Hey, would you mind if I borrowed the mountain loft for a weekend? Maybe she'll spend a couple of nights there with me."

"Over my dead body," Adam snapped and then shook his head as he realized he'd walked straight into a trap.

Matt threw his head back and laughed. "Relax, brother. I'm not interested in her." His tone changed. "You are, damn it. You like the woman. Do something about it."

"You know that's not a possibility." Adam refused to look at him.

"I know you think it's not an option. You're wrong. The past is in the past. Leave it there. Let go, mate. You've had enough pain in your life. It's time to move on."

Adam shot him an acid look. He didn't speak. Matt knew the pain hadn't passed. It never would.

"Your life didn't end ten years ago."

"Yes," Adam said, his voice as dead as his heart. "It did."

"You have a chance to start over. Something's telling you it's time, and you know it. Otherwise, you wouldn't have reacted this way to Lexi. You would just have filed her away with all the other numbers."

Shit, Matt's words made sense. He reacted differently to Lexi. He couldn't cut her out of his thoughts or his life. Something made him go back to her, repeatedly.

"Adam, give her a chance. Give yourself a chance."

He shook his head again. "I can't do that."

"Why not?"

They both knew the answer. Adam pursed his lips and remained silent. He didn't quite trust his voice.

"You scared?" Only Matt would have the audacity to ask.

He grimaced. Yes, goddamn it. He was frigging terrified.

"Same old story, huh? You get involved, you get hurt."

Shit, what did Matt think? That he was a selfish git? "Not just me, mate."

"Ah." Matt nodded. "You're worried you're going to break her heart. Very chivalrous of you."

The sarcasm was not lost on him. He resisted the urge to swear at his friend.

"She's an adult woman," Matt said. "She can make decisions for herself."

Yes, Lexi was indeed an adult woman. He'd become intimately acquainted with just how adult she was. That didn't mean letting her into his life was the right decision.

"We're different. We want different things out of life."

Matt looked surprised. "You know her well enough to know what she wants from her future?"

Damn. He had an answer for everything, didn't he? "I know her well enough to know what's important to her." He didn't have to be a rocket scientist to see what mattered to Lexi. People did. Lexi cared, AJ didn't. Not anymore. That made for irreconcilable differences.

"You don't have to have similar beliefs and thoughts to get on."

"There has to be some common ground," Adam countered.

"Mutual attraction isn't common ground?"

That stumped him. He and Lexi shared a mutual attraction. He had no idea if she liked him but he was certain she was attracted to him. His body stirred and he subtly shifted the newspaper onto his lap before he embarrassed himself. "Mutual attraction doesn't last."

"It doesn't have to. I'm not asking you to marry the woman. I'm asking you to give her a chance. See where it goes."

For a good few minutes, Adam remained silent. He wanted to give Lexi a chance, wanted to see where it would go, yet the very idea scared him shitless. What if she demanded things he couldn't give? What if she began to care for him? Worse, what if he began to care about her?

Rubbing his hands over his perpetually tired eyes, he gave up. "Can I agree to think about it for now?" he asked, keen for Matt to drop the subject.

"Can you promise to do that?"

"If I do, can we change the subject?"

"We'll talk about the Melbourne deal," Matt agreed.

"Then I promise to think about it."

Matt assessed him carefully, then nodded. "Lewin agreed to the price but he wasn't altogether happy with the conditions attached. He wants affirmation that none of his staff will be compromised."

"I can't give him any guarantees."

"Give him something. He's giving you his company."

Adam considered his request. "Right. Three months trial period. I'll guarantee every job for three months. It's up to each individual to prove his or her worth in that time. More than that I won't offer."

"Sounds fair. We'll run it by Lewin at the meeting." He leaned forward and took out the in-flight magazine. "Interesting..." He flipped a page. "Very interesting..." Another page. "Hmmm..."

"Okay," Adam finally snapped. "What the bloody hell is so interesting?"

"I'm thinking, you're giving a bunch of complete strangers a real chance, an opportunity to prove themselves, and yet..."

He knew he'd regret asking. "And yet?"

"And yet you're not willing to give Lexi a second thought."

"Change the subject."

"Sure." Matt flipped another page of the magazine. "This is the easy part of the negotiations. All I need is a signature. Pretty simple, yeah?"

"Yeah."

"Right. So remind me again what you're doing here?"

Crap. Matt wasn't going to let this rest. He knew his reason for going to Melbourne had nothing to do with business. He just needed to get away from Sydney. Needed to put some space between himself and Lexi before he did something irrational. "Matt?"

"Yeah?"

"Let it go."

"You'll think about it?"

"I said I would."

"I'll let it go." This time, he did.

Adam tried to focus on the headlines but his concentration was shot. Promising Matt he'd think about Lexi hadn't been hard. Forcing himself not to think about her was damn near impossible.

∞

Adam stared dumbfounded at the woman standing before

him. Christ, what was she doing in Melbourne? Furthermore, what were the odds of bumping into her on the street like this?

"Tracey?" Apart from looking a couple years older, she'd hardly changed. A few lines around her eyes, a different hairstyle and perhaps an air of maturity that hadn't been there before.

"Don't look so shocked, Adam," she said. "It's just me."

Just me? Did she have the foggiest idea what seeing "just her" did to him? It wrenched his heart and twisted his stomach and tortured his mind.

"What are you doing in Melbourne?" He had to stop coming to this city. Every time he did he bumped into a woman who shook him to his bones.

"I'm here on business."

"Business?" She hadn't been working last time he'd seen her.

"Yes. I've started up a clothing line for children."

Logical choice. She had an eye for fashion and a way with children. "How's it going?"

"It's doing well in Perth, now I'm trying to bring the label to Melbourne."

"And?"

"So far, so good. If the line proves successful here, I'll go to Sydney next."

"Good luck. I hope it works out." He did. He just didn't want her in Sydney.

"Thanks. What are you doing here? I thought the business mogul never left his office." Her voice held no malice, just gentle teasing.

"We're purchasing a company here."

"Are you still driving yourself so hard?"

Sure, the concern in her voice touched him—she was the one person who understood why he drove himself the way he did. Didn't mean he wanted to stand around and chat. His mind already searched for an escape, an excuse to leave before she started asking questions.

"Hey, you know how it is," he answered casually. "When there's work to be done, someone's got to do it."

"I spoke to your mother the other day," Tracey said. "She's worried about you. She said you're involved with another cancer charity."

Fuck, couldn't they just make polite conversation about the weather or something? They hadn't seen each other in years. Did she have to drive to the heart of the problem within two minutes of meeting him again?

"I'm not involved. Someone approached me and I gave her the money. That's all. Matt's doing the follow-up."

She touched his arm, left her hand there. "Even now you're not able to move on, are you?"

He simply was not prepared to go there. "How is my mother? Do you still see her so regularly?"

Her brow puckered and she frowned. "We meet every few months. I like the contact and so does she. We both find it comforting."

"Yeah, Mum always did like you." Then, because he had to ask—even if it damn near killed him—he said, "How is your family? How are the boys doing?"

She gave him a sad smile. "They're wonderful. Getting big now. Jason's already five and Corey's going to be three next month."

Adam knew that. He made it a rule never to forget their

birthdays. Sent them gifts every year.

"You should come and meet them sometime."

Enough. He had to get away. "I'm sure I will. One day," he said as he checked his watch. "Is that the time? My next meeting starts in ten minutes and it's three blocks away. I have to run."

She frowned again, her eyes filled with hurt and sympathy.

"Hey," he said and impulsively hugged her. "It's good to see you again." He surprised himself by meaning it. It was nice seeing her. It just wasn't nice remembering everything he associated with her.

She hugged him, squeezing him close for a minute. "You too, Ad. Take care." She stepped back. "I mean that. Look after yourself."

Adam nodded, gave a tight smile and walked off.

"Send my love to Matt," she called after him and he lifted his arm in acknowledgement.

Her gaze cut into his back long after he'd turned the corner and walked out of her line of vision.

Chapter Ten

Lexi's footsteps echoed through the empty offices, the odour of fresh paint sharp in her nose. The walls were now a mint green, the color chosen specifically for its soothing hue. She didn't need to close her eyes to picture the place furnished. The couches and armchairs were being delivered on Monday week—plump, inviting seats with bold, bright prints that would appeal to kids of all ages.

The new coordinator would also arrive on the same Monday. After extensive interviews, Lexi'd found the perfect person to head up the program: Abbey Perkins, a young, dynamic social worker.

Someone knocked on the door and she turned to the sound, expecting it. Matt had scheduled a meeting and she was excited to update him on the progress.

Only it wasn't Matt who stood in the doorway.

Adam.

He looked quite devastating.

He'd removed his suit jacket and tie and rolled his sleeves up to his elbows. Black hair covered his muscular lower arms and peeked over his shirt collar. A five o'clock shadow darkened his jaw and upper lip, and his icy eyes flashed in his tanned skin.

Her stomach lurched.

She hadn't heard from him since the wedding, more than two weeks ago. In that time, he'd driven her completely bananas. Or rather, her thoughts of him had driven her crazy. Something had changed at the wedding. They'd managed to shelve the antagonism, managed to turn the attraction into something sweet and sexy instead of something cheap and ugly. They'd become...friends. Sure, the bond was fragile. Still, it was there. She'd found she genuinely liked him, and unless she'd misread him completely, she'd thought he'd begun to like her too.

So why the freaking hell hadn't he phoned? A simple hello would have sufficed, although a marathon session in bed—or out—would have been preferable.

She didn't get him. One minute he'd act as frigid as his cold blue eyes, and the next, hotter than his naked chest. When he was plain Adam, with his traffic-stopping smile and gentle humor, she melted into a puddle on the floor in front of him.

He was an enigma. What went on his head? He'd kissed and seduced her, and then demeaned and belittled her. He'd chased her away, and then begged her to return. He'd mocked her strategy, and then supported her ideas. He'd, well...he'd just driven her bananas.

What about the trauma buried in his eyes? She'd noticed it twice, and both times the ill-concealed pain left her reeling. Matt hadn't just helped him through a "rough patch". Anyone who housed so much sorrow, who hid so much grief, had to have been through hell.

Her heart ached for him. She longed to offer him comfort. Where would she begin? How could she soothe his pain when he wouldn't let her in?

"Adam." She groped around for a casual greeting, which

Jess Dee

wasn't easy considering the startling array of backflips and somersaults her stomach performed. "You've caught me by surprise. I expected Matt."

"He...couldn't make it today. I came in his place."

Bless the forces that kept him away. "I thought you'd decided to have nothing more to do with the program?"

"I had." He shrugged. "Someone had to come and I was available."

So she had about an hour with him. She had no idea how she'd manage to spend that time without imaging him naked, but she'd damn well give it her best shot.

"How have you been?" she asked, determined to not to think about his awesome abs or his erect penis. She absolutely would not picture him making love to her. That would screw with her powers of concentration.

"Good, you?"

I waited around for days for you to phone and pretended not to be disappointed when you didn't. For a while I thought maybe, just maybe, there could be something between us. I guess I was wrong.

"I'm good too," she said as he pushed his hand through his hair, leaving it mussed and standing up a little.

Her heart did a three-point turn. That's exactly how his hair had looked in the hotel, after the second time he'd come. He'd run his hands through it, stared at her with glazed eyes and said, "Christ, that was unbelievable".

Aw, crap. She'd imagined them doing it. Not good. "Would you like to start by going over recent accomplishments? Or would you prefer a tour of the offices, seeing as you're here anyway?" Blood roared through her ears and though she watched his lips move, she didn't hear his answer. How could she? She was reliving the best sex of her life.

She was back in the hotel, panting on the bed, shivering as he bent down to lick her between the legs. Heat stirred in her belly and snaked outwards. Her cheeks burned, as did her breasts. The potent flames of arousal scorched every part of her. He lapped up the moisture that ran down her inner thighs, spread her lips with his thumbs and dipped his tongue in to taste her. Then he reached up and sucked sweetly on her sensitive nub. She lay on the bed, her arm flung over her eyes, her thigh wrapped around his neck. His tongue. Oh, God, the things he could do with his tongue. She keened softly under his ministrations.

"Lexi?" Adam stepped forward, jerking her back to the present. He stood close, with his hand on her arm, burning through her sleeve. She focused on his mouth, watched his lips move, saw a flash of pink tongue between his white teeth. The same pink tongue that had flung her headfirst into the throws of ecstasy.

She bit her lower lip, her mouth bone-dry, and he growled and dropped his arm.

"I...I'm sorry. I have a lot on my mind." She forced herself to look into his eyes, wondering how he'd respond if she kissed him. She wanted to kiss him. Sweet Lord, she wanted to kiss him. Wanted to sip from the mouth that had given her such pleasure.

His face was a dark mask and she didn't dare.

For a full minute, neither of them spoke. They simply stood, watching each other. Lexi knew her cheeks were flushed and her breath was uneven. She struggled to still her pounding heart. He knew, read her thoughts. Hadn't he told her he recognized the signs of her arousal?

Did he have any telltale signs? Would he be aroused,

knowing she was? She studied him. There were signs all right. They just weren't of desire. Beneath his tanned skin he looked pale. The whites of his eyes were bloodshot and frown lines crowded his mouth. Although still ridiculously sexy, he looked tired and stressed and he held his shoulders in a stiff line.

"Hey," she said in a gentle voice, "you okay?" Tension radiated off him in waves. If she hadn't been so involved in her memories, she'd have noticed it sooner.

Adam glanced around the room and cleared his throat. "Hospitals make me uncomfortable."

She sensed a wealth of unspoken thoughts. Adam wasn't just uncomfortable here, he hated everything about the place. "A lot of people feel ill at ease in hospitals," she said empathically. Why was it so hard for him to be here? Had he had a bad experience in hospital? Had he been sick?

His smile was tight. "How about you give me that tour? The less time I spend here, the better."

Ouch. She knew he was talking about the hospital but she couldn't help taking the comment personally. He was here because he had no choice. Matt couldn't make it, so he came instead. Not to see her—to check out the program.

She guided him through the rooms, bringing them to life as she detailed their future furnishings and functions to him.

"And last of all," she said as she led him into the cramped room with the sink and counter, "this will be the kitchen. We'll add a kettle and microwave, and we'll fill the shelves with plates and cutlery and the fridge with drinks and snacks. The kids can help themselves anytime. We'll put the fridge in that corner—" she turned to point and lost her train of thought.

The room was small with the two of them squeezed into it. They stood so close they almost touched. Adam made no pretence of looking where she pointed. He pinned his gaze on her mouth, his eyes hot and hungry. His lips parted and he swallowed hard as she stared back at him. The desire in his expression took her breath away.

Lack of oxygen almost choked her and she inhaled deeply then let the air escape in soft shudders. Lord, what this man did to her with only a look. If he would just reach out and touch her now, she'd surrender herself to him in a heartbeat. Here in the kitchen, in the middle of the hospital, she would kick the door shut and claw his clothes off and tear her own away and just let him fuck her.

"Lexi," his voice was gruff.

"Adam," she whispered back.

Silently, he stared at her mouth. Her eyelids grew heavy and fluttered closed. She hung there, suspended in the tiny room, waiting. The sound of their breathing drowned the noises outside. She floated toward him, her body pulled by an invisible magnet. Her lips parted slightly and she knew it was just a matter of time before his mouth touched hers, his tongue sought hers. Her heart raced and gooseflesh skittered up her spine. Blood pooled—

"I've seen enough here. Let's get on with it."

Lexi blinked in shock. What the...?

Flecks of ice glinted in his eyes. She gaped at him, mortified. Talk about misreading a situation. Unable to take the mockery on his face a second longer, she pushed past him and called over her shoulder, "If you'll come with me, I have a list of issues to discuss in my office."

The quicker they got there, the quicker they could get this meeting over and done with. She practically raced through the lounge and into the hospital corridor. If the floor opened up and swallowed her now, she'd face her fate happily. Of course, that wouldn't happen. Nothing ever happened the way she wanted it to with Riley around.

Once in her office, she closed the door and invited him to sit down. He declined, electing rather to lean against the wall, one foot crossed over the other. She stood behind her desk and briefly consulted her folder. Not that she needed reminders about today's agenda. It just gave her somewhere to look other than his face. She refused to let him see how much his rejection threw her.

She shoved aside any thoughts about preliminary discussions, loath to prolong her time with Riley. Instead, she launched straight into the facts. "We've accomplished a fair amount since last I met with Matt. In summary, I've hired a program manager. She's a social worker with a medical background. The furniture is due to arrive the week after next and the promotional material has been distributed to the wards and the reception area. We've set up a media interview for the Wednesday three weeks from now." She paused to take a deep breath. *"Matt* will be attending that."

The words tumbled out of her mouth; she couldn't talk fast enough. If she could finish this meeting, she could get him the hell out of her office. Then she would afford herself the luxury of curling into a tiny ball on the floor and squirming in embarrassment. "The doors open officially the following Monday, after the staff establish a formal agenda and program. Abbey Perkins, the new manager, will run a five-day training program for all staff members and volunteers involved. That will take place in two weeks' time. We already have three children enrolled in the program, siblings of patients currently in hospital. The ward has been primed with information, and referrals have started trickling in from them. We've taken out advertisements in women's and health magazines as well as a couple of medical journals and publications found in doctors' rooms and pharmacies. Slowly, the word is circulating."

She finally looked at him, ensuring she wore a vacant expression on her face.

She'd be damned if she let him see how bent out of shape she was. "That is it in a nutshell. Any questions?"

Without answering, he pushed himself off the wall and took seven—she counted each one of them—very slow, very calculated steps in her direction. His face was unreadable, hypnotic, she couldn't tear her eyes away. He walked past her desk. Unsure of his intentions, she swallowed a tiny gasp as he stopped a mere heartbeat away from her.

The hunger was back in his expression, just as it had been in the kitchen. Only this time, she refused to fall for it. Once bitten...! She took a step back, creating a little space between them. Wrong move. Her butt touched the desktop and she was trapped, caught between a slab of wood and a wall of muscle.

He stepped closer and inhaled slowly. When he exhaled, his breath mingled with hers, sending a wave of longing shimmering through her. His aftershave tickled her nose and she made a concerted effort to hold herself down, to not reach over and bury her face in his chest and gasp in his masculine scent.

Desire overrode her aggravation. Need pulsed through her, so powerful it rendered her muscles useless. She stood paralyzed, aching for his touch.

Her lids grew heavy. She fought every impulse to close them, fought the temptation to tilt her head slightly backward and offer him her mouth as she had in the kitchen.

"Look, Adam—"

Before she could finish, he swooped in and kissed her.

His lips enveloped hers and his tongue took complete possession of her mouth. It delved inside, hot and wet and demanding. And sweet. Oh, so sweet. Waves of pleasure spiraled through her. Her toes curled and her stomach quivered and she almost wept at the relief she found in his arms as they wrapped around her, pulling her against him.

She surrendered to him completely. Her mouth relaxed and her lips responded and she accepted his searching tongue, feasting on it. Flesh burning and breasts tingling, need rolled over her hard and fast, and she clung to him.

She curved herself into him, flattening her breasts against the solid mass of muscle that was his chest, fitting her hips around his groin so his erection pressed into her belly. She kissed him and kissed him and kissed him, until finally, breathless, he tugged his lips away from hers and rested his forehead on hers.

"Christ," he said, "I've waited a long time to do that."

"Adam..."

"Come away with me, Lexi. Tonight. I have a place in the Blue Mountains. It's wild and it's beautiful, and I'd like to share it with you."

She pulled away from him, confusion and frustration winning out over desire. One minute he rejected her cold, the next he kissed her senseless. Now he wanted her to go away with him?

"One weekend, Lexi. All I ask of you is this one weekend."

She shook her head, dizzy from the staggering effects of his kiss and the emotions whirling about in her stomach. "I don't get you." She pressed the palms of her hands into her eyes and pushed down hard, as if the action would somehow clear her jumbled thoughts. "I don't understand what's going on inside that head of yours. Five minutes ago I embarrassed myself stupid waiting for you to kiss me, and you weren't interested. Now you want me to spend a weekend with you. I just don't get you."

"You think I wasn't interested back there?" He snorted and clasped her hand in his, pulling it away from her face. "You think I haven't wanted to touch you since I walked into those rooms and saw you?" He moved her hand down and placed it on his groin.

He was hard, so very hard. The need to act on his arousal overwhelmed her, whipping the air from her lungs.

"Hell, woman, I look at you and I get an erection."

She molded her hand to him, her mouth hungry to taste his again. He felt so good, so real. She caressed him, ran her fingers over the rigid outline of his cock, and he growled.

"The first time I saw you I wanted to kiss you." He drew in a ragged breath, reached out and traced first one heaving breast and then the other. "I wanted you, full stop. I wanted to touch your body and taste your lips and bury myself in your hot, moist center." His eyes were hooded and his voice was low and deep and soft, so soft that if someone stood behind her, they wouldn't hear. "I thought sleeping with you would take care of it. That I wouldn't need you any more." He settled his lips against the tender spot below her ear, then nibbled his way up her lobe and whispered, "I was wrong."

She should move, should push his hand away. They were in her office. Anyone could walk in. She had neither the strength nor the inclination to do so. Instead, she remained where she was, pinned down by his mouth, helpless to fight him. She squirmed as another wave of longing washed over her.

"Making love to you just made me want you more. I can't sleep for wanting you. I lie in bed at night and crave the weight of your body on top of mine. I want to see you naked and aroused in front of me. I want to hear you moan and scream my name. I want you so hot from my touch that you burn inside. Like I do. Night after excruciating night."

Oh God, did any man have a right to talk like this? She was at work, for heaven's sake. *Pull yourself together. Push him away.* She would, she vowed, just as soon as she found the energy to voice her thoughts.

Keeping his lips close to her ear, he breathed, "Come away with me, Lexi. Let me make love to you tonight. Let me hold you and touch you."

If her body answered, if she responded on gut instinct alone, she'd accept. She'd simply wind her arms around his neck and let the man carry her out of her office and straight to his car. *If.*

Somewhere, a small part of her brain still functioned normally and it focused on one sentence. *All I ask of you is this one weekend.*

She couldn't do it. She knew she was nuts. A weekend away with Adam. A weekend of wild, uninhibited sex with the world's most gorgeous man. What more could a woman ask for?

A chance, that's what. A chance to get to know him. A chance to give whatever sparked between them time to ignite— and not just in bed. Adam intrigued her; she couldn't keep away. She wanted—no, she needed—to find out everything about him. His past, his present, what made him into the man he was and what he had been through that caused him such pain. And why, *why*, her attraction to him was so powerful that no matter how many times he pushed her away, she kept coming back for more?

A weekend of carefree sex would hardly give her that chance. She couldn't do it. She couldn't go. It was time to acknowledge that when it came to relationships, Lexi wanted the world. She wanted what Sarah had. She wanted what Daniel had. A weekend away wasn't going to cut it. Not by a long shot. Nothing less than a whole lot of honest-to-goodness, real-life time spent in each other's company would do.

He offered forty-eight hours.

Using every ounce of available energy, she dropped her arm and pulled back from the hand that trailed an exquisite path over the upper curves of her breasts. "I'm sorry, Adam." She shook her head. "I just can't do it."

Chapter Eleven

Adam changed down from fifth to fourth gear, and then down again to third. The BMW purred as it decreased speed, hugging the curves of the twisting mountain road. With the roof down, the wind whipped through the car, pure and fresh and strongly tinged with the pungent scent of eucalyptus.

He glanced at her, flashed his traffic-stopping smile. "I'm pleased you came."

"So am I." She wrinkled her nose.

"I didn't think you would."

"I wasn't going to." Approximately thirty seconds after refusing his invitation, she'd realized she made a mistake. She'd wanted a chance? Well, what did she think his invitation offered? Yeah, it may only be for forty-eight hours, but what had she expected? A marriage proposal? Two days alone together was a great start. If she played her cards right, it might turn into a lot longer.

"What made you change your mind?"

She shot him a wicked look. "What do you think?"

The traffic stopper returned. "I have a confession."

For someone in the process of owning up to something, he didn't look particularly guilty. "Am I going to want to hear this?"

"Matt could have made it to the meeting this afternoon."

"What?"

"I asked him not come."

"You did?" *Yes.*

"I had to see you, Lexi." The teasing quality in his voice was gone. "I'm going to Hong Kong on Tuesday for two weeks. I couldn't leave here without resolving things between us."

"Is that what I am to you? An unresolved issue?"

He didn't respond.

"So spending a weekend with me will help you find...an answer to your problem?" She held no false illusions. He'd designed this weekend to work her out of his system. Period. She should be pissed but how could she be angry when his problem was the fact that she was in his system to begin with?

He slowed down and turned off the highway onto a narrow country road. "Woman, until I have you naked and alone, I won't be able to resolve one damn thing."

A lick of desire shot through her. She closed her eyes, rested her head on the headrest and stroked his thigh. The muscles rippled in his leg. "Care to tell me how you intend resolving things?"

His tone dropped a notch. "Sure you want to hear?"

She dragged her hand down to his knee and back up again. "Uh huh."

He released the gearshift and clasped her hand, effectively stopping her movement. "First off, I'm going to try and not drive us clear off the mountain." He wound his fingers through hers. "It's tough concentrating with a raging erection."

She twisted her head to look at his lap. Sure enough, she could see why his concentration might be compromised. Distinctly pleased with herself, she smiled and stretched. "What *can* you do with a raging erection?"

He turned to look at her with an arched eyebrow. "For starters, I can make you very, very happy."

She leaned back and closed her eyes again, trying not to smile. "I'm sure you can. What about after that?"

"I can make you even happier."

She snorted at the sheer arrogance in his voice. "And then?"

He brought her hand to his mouth and kissed her palm. "You can make me very happy."

"That's it? That's the best you got?" Oh, she wasn't disappointed, not by a long shot. She knew he would make her very, very, happy. Then she'd return the favor. Tenfold. Still, she knew for a fact he could do better.

"Are you challenging me?"

"No, I'm just remembering, that's all."

"Remembering what?"

"Me. You. In your office."

He was silent.

"I'm standing in your office, bent over your desk." She kept her eyes shut, drawn back by the memory of his description. "The door's locked, you don't want anyone walking in, catching us like this. My skirt's bunched up high over my hips and I'm looking out the window, staring at the view. I can't really see it. I can't see much, because I know you're standing behind me, staring at my ass."

Ooh, she was getting into this. "Your gaze burns into my buttocks. It's making me so hot, I start to shake." She was getting very into this. "I want you to touch me. Want you to tear off my thong. I don't care where it lands as long as it's not in the way anymore. You're surprised at the color. You thought it would be black and lacy. It's not. It's deep purple, just like my bra."

Was he enjoying this as much as she was? She opened an eye to look at him and caught the pained expression on his face. "You can't decide how to get rid of it. With your hands or your teeth? Your indecision drives me mad. I'm so wet, juices drip onto my thong every time you breathe." She closed her eyes and sank deeper into the seat. "What is taking so long? I picture you kneeling behind me, taking the lace between your teeth and dragging the panties over my hips and down my legs. You run your wet, warm tongue up my inner thigh and then dip it between my legs and groan. I groan too."

"Lexi..." Adam's voice was rough but it trailed off, and she continued.

"You don't use your mouth. Instead, you hook your thumb on the thong and use your hands to take it off. After that, you do nothing. You simply stand behind me, staring. Again, your gaze burns me. This time it's not on my ass. It's between my legs, and knowing you watch me so intimately makes me even wetter." Never mind his office, she was wet now, sitting in his car. "I know you see the cream trickling down my thigh, know you're turned on. You're already aroused. Now you're getting uncomfortable. Your cock gets harder, your pants tighter. You want to touch me, want to dip into all that cream. You'd start with one finger but when you realize how hot I really am for you, you'd dip another one in, and then another. You'd roll your thumb over my clit, massage it while you fucked me with your fingers until I couldn't take it anymore, and I'd come."

Although the roof was down and the wind forceful enough to keep her cool, Lexi was ablaze. She'd burned when Adam had spun the same story for her and she burned using it to seduce him now. She undid the top button of her blouse.

Adam swore softly beside her.

In his office, his words had been tinged with bitterness. He'd used them as a weapon against her. Now that the war was over, she'd take his fantasy and turn it into reality. A highly pleasurable reality that would obliterate any leftover animosity.

She sighed. "You don't use your hands, do you? You know another way of making me come. One that will be infinitely more pleasurable for both of us. By this time, I'm so horny I shove my ass back in the air, practically begging you to do whatever the hell it is you want to do, just wishing you'd do something. I'm so...empty, so needy. Why won't you touch me? I growl at the sheer frustration that courses through me." She gave a soft snarl.

Adam's breath was erratic. He murmured nonsensically beside her.

"Even though I can't see you, I know you're smiling, wallowing in your power over me. I'm putty in your hands. At last, you place your palm on the small of my back and push me down against the surface of your desk. My breasts are swollen and aching, and I rub them against the smooth wood. It doesn't help. It's not the wood I want. It's your flesh, your hands and your mouth, caressing them, kissing them, sucking on my nipples. I moan and wriggle my ass some more. Touch me, goddamn it. Why won't you touch me?"

Lexi gulped in air. "There's a noise. It's the sound of your shoes hitting the floor, the shuffle as you remove your pants. Your hands close over my hips, and I want to scream I'm so relieved. You pull me back, position me just so. You don't need to do anything else to prepare me, because I am so ready for you. The tip of your cock brushes against the back of my thigh, grazes my lips. I swear, if it touches my clit, I'll break. I'm so aroused, your slightest movement will send me over the edge."

Lexi's own reality blurred. She tried to stay in the present, tried to remind herself that this fantasy was for Adam, not for her. It was impossible. She'd submerged herself completely in his fantasy and her words.

"Just when I think I can't take it a minute longer, you plunge into me, fill me with one thrust of your hips. The sensation. Oh, sweet Lord, the sensation. Words can't describe it. I scream out and you pull back and plunge into me again, and then again. Your legs are plastered against mine, your hips cradle my ass. I want to weep it's so damn good. Your cock is so deep inside me, it's hard to tell where you end and I begin. We're one person. You plunge in again and again. Oh, Adam... I can't take it. It's too... I'm falling apart. I'm going to come. You move, twist inside me, and... God help me, I'm coming. Oh...Oh...Adam. Oh. My. God."

She panted—she couldn't help it. Beside her, Adam drew in a sharp breath.

"You're about to come too, you can't stop it. You fuck me hard, once, twice, and then you freeze. Only for a second. You explode, spurting your come into me. You call my name, spurt again and again. I'm shivering. You're panting. 'Christ, Lexi'. You want to say more but you can't. I'm exhausted. I collapse on the desk, grateful there's something there to support me. You collapse on top of me, spent, and I relish your weight, your heat on my back. Your cock is still in me, still twitching, sending shivers of pleasure racing through me. For a long while, all we can do is lie there, listening to the sound of our breathing."

She opened her eyes and looked at Adam. "That's okay. For now that's the only place I want to be."

The car had stopped. At some point, he must have pulled over to the side of the road. His eyes flamed. The ice in them had melted away.

"Lexi," his voice sounded like gravel. "I have never fucked someone on the side of the road before. But I swear to you, if you say one more word, I will haul you out of this car, throw you over the hood and live out every word of that fantasy, right here, right now." He swore. "Got it?"

She practically purred in her seat. "I'm so wet, Adam. That little scenario's got me all worked up." She undid another two buttons and slipped her hand into her blouse.

A muscle ticked in his cheek. "This road is deserted. No one uses it apart from me." He dragged his breath in. "Believe me, Lexi, I do not make idle threats."

Good. Her stomach lurched as she stroked an aroused nipple. "Damn, I'm glad I didn't wear a bra."

"Open your shirt." It was an order, not a request. "All the way."

With her free hand, she did as he said until the blouse hung open, revealing her braless breasts. "My nipples have been rubbing against the inside of the shirt," she told him. "The soft caress of cotton is torture when all I want is the firm touch of your hand, the wet probing of your lips." She tweaked her nipple and moaned, then touched her other breast.

He watched her, swallowed hard. "Your belt. Take it off."

Leaving her hand on her breast, she unbuckled her belt, freeing it from her jeans. There was not another man in the world she'd do this for. Not out in the open, exposed for anyone to see.

"Now the button," he rasped.

She raked her nipple, moaned again and undid the button. Only Adam. He was the only man she trusted enough. He nodded and motioned her to continue. She slid the zip down, aware of the irony of her trust. How could she know she was safe in his hands, when he'd shared almost nothing of himself with her?

"Are you going to do it, Adam? Are you going to fuck me here, on the side of the road?" Traffic from the main road was muted by distance. All around, nature called. Kookaburras laughed from hidden branches, a magpie cawed to its mate, and the wind rustled through the leaves of the surrounding trees. She could hardly keep still. Anticipation hummed through her veins. Would he do it? Would she let him do it?

"Take them off." His eyes trained on her waist, on the hand that rested on her bare stomach.

She kicked off her shoes, lifted her butt and pushed her pants over her hips. "The thought is making me even hotter. I want you to, Adam." Oh, she'd let him all right—and hopefully, in return he'd put a little trust in her too. "I want you to bend me over the car and take me." She shimmied out of her jeans, leaving them in a pile at her feet. Shifting her legs a little, she ran her finger between them, tracing a line from her lips to her clit and back again. "Wet," she muttered thickly.

"Get out of the car." He sounded tortured.

She complied, opening her door and climbing out. Her body rejoiced in the freedom of space and she stretched languorously.

"Should I leave my panties on?" she asked, looking at him over her shoulder. By his expression, she assumed he was in no state to answer. A smile of sheer, feminine satisfaction tugged at her lips. Casually, she bent over and removed them, dropping them on the seat before taking a step so she stood at the side of the trunk.

She rested her bottom on it. The metallic paint warmed her buttocks, and the breeze cooled her bare flesh. "You coming to join me?" she asked without turning around. The sound of the door creaking was answer enough.

Expectation crackled between them. Blood pumped through her veins and need flared in her belly. She touched first one breast then the other, let her head drop back and her eyes close. Ran her hand down until it skimmed over the neatly trimmed thatch on her mound and made its way lower. She touched herself and groaned. Her lips were slick, moisture coating them, and she dipped inside and groaned again.

Footsteps crunched against the leaves on the ground beside the car, and then silence. He stood before her.

"In your office that day, I was so hot. You got me all worked up and I was so ready. I wanted you to take me, to fuck me like you'd said you would." She shook her head, remembered the frustration that had rippled through her at the time. Remembered the anger in his voice. "You didn't...you never... All you did was apologize." She opened her eyes, looked at him. His shirt was unbuttoned and hung loose. His heavy, hooded gaze focused on her hand. "I didn't just want your apology, Adam. I wanted your touch, too." She wanted more than that now. She wanted everything he had to give her.

She slipped her finger out, and then pushed it back in again. "Aaah." It took a few seconds before she could talk. "I still want your touch. But I... I can't wait."

"Give me your hand, Lexi." She heard the effort it took for him to speak.

She reached for him with her free hand.

"Not that one."

Reluctantly, she withdrew and held it out to him. He closed his hand around hers, lifted it to his mouth and then licked her with his exquisitely warm tongue. Slowly, gently, he licked. First the nail and then the tip, and then he drew the whole finger into his mouth and suckled.

She cried out and he released her, guided her hand back

between her legs.

"Touch yourself, sweetheart. I want..." He swallowed. "I want to watch you come."

Oh. Sweet Lord. She wouldn't make a minute. How could she touch herself while he watched and manage to stretch out the pleasure? Impossible. She dipped her hand between her lower lips, watched his mouth open and close, and pulled back out.

Sensation fizzed inside. Her lips were swollen, her groin sensitized. The look in his eyes as he watched her was possibly the most arousing thing she'd ever witnessed. Moisture dripped onto her hand and she used it to massage her clit.

"Adam. I'm...I'm so...horny." Her voice caught as she struggled to speak. "Look what you do to me. Your eyes...watching me." It was impossible to form whole sentences. "Makes me...heady, hot." She fucked herself again, did it several times in a row. "I'm thinking of your cock." Oh, she wanted it now. Wanted it deep, deep inside. She massaged her clit again. "I want it." She licked her lips and massaged a little harder, aware of the sensation building up, the throbbing between her legs, the breathlessness. Aware of his eyes on her.

"Watch me, Adam," she gasped. "Watch me, I'm going to come." Liquid gushed as the sensation peaked. Pressure crowned and waves rippled over her. "Adam, oh God, look what you made me do." She rubbed frantically as the orgasm rolled through her, the tremors carrying on longer than she'd expected. It was Adam. Watching her. The gratification it evoked was almost as heady as the rush of her climax.

"Christ, Lexi." The words sounded as if they'd been torn from his throat.

Before the waves had time to settle, he put his hands on her hips. He pulled her off the car, flipped her round and pushed her shoulders down—just like their fantasy. Her breasts squashed against the trunk, her ass poked into the air. Her nether lips still pulsed from her orgasm, gleaming up at him.

The heat from the car warmed her nipples, soothed her breasts. She heard the rip of foil, felt his pants as they swished down his legs, and there he was, pushing into her, filling her. She'd craved this, worked hard for it. This and so much more. He readily surrendered his body to her—would he surrender his emotions as well? What about his past?

She gasped as he entered her, desire exploding within like giant fireworks. There was no time to adapt to his presence, to shift to accommodate him. He slammed into her hard and fast, repeatedly, his balls slapping against her.

"Oh, God, Adam," she yelled. Rational thought became impossible. She wanted to connect with him on a deeper level—sex honestly wasn't the only thing she desired from him. But at this point in time, it was the only thing she could focus on, the only thing she needed.

Before, her orgasm had been gentle, rippling through her in soft tremors. This one blindsided her. It came on swift and powerful and sent her into violent spasms of pleasure. She screamed as the euphoria engulfed her, as waves crashed around her, deafening her to everything but the sound of Adam's moans. She screamed again as her inner walls clenched around him, nerve-endings igniting in a fire of pleasure, demanding his release. He gave it to her, his orgasm as wild and uninhibited as hers.

When it was over, he collapsed on top of her, and the two of them lay on the BMW, dazed in the aftermath of their passion. Adam's chest pressed into her back. With no small measure of satisfaction, Lexi registered the synchronized pounding of their hearts. She'd successfully shared his fantasy, turned it into a very pleasurable reality. Perhaps now he might share more of himself with her, maybe even reveal his secrets to her.

CR

As the last rim of golden fire dipped below the line of trees on the horizon, leaving a pale orange and pink glow bathing the leaves in an ethereal light, Adam took a sip of scotch and looked at Lexi. She stood beside him, leaning against the rail of the balcony.

"It's breathtaking," she whispered, as though loath to disturb the tranquility that descended around them.

Birdcalls faded with the sun, and in their place frogs chirped noisily. The leaves rustled in the breeze and the calm of the evening enveloped him. Here he could be himself. Here he could let down his defenses and let go of his anger and his sadness and simply enjoy living. It was the only place he found any peace.

"I'm glad you like it." The wind played with her hair, sending tendrils floating around her face.

"I've been transported to another world. There's no one around for miles, is there?"

"Think I would have pulled over earlier if there was?" They shared a private smile and Adam tried unsuccessfully to ignore the intimacy of the moment. "Katoomba's about a twenty minute drive from here and the closest neighbors are five kilometers away. I like the isolation."

"It's a perfect place to escape. You must come out here every weekend."

He shrugged. "I come when I find the time. It's not as often as I'd like." If he managed to get here once every two months, it was a lot. This weekend he'd had to come and he'd had to bring

143

Lexi with him. His chance meeting with Tracey had dredged up old memories and left him shaken. For the last ten days, loneliness had descended on him like a thick, grey cloud. This morning he'd experienced a compulsive need to squelch his self-imposed isolation. Just for a weekend.

The hurt was always there. Always lurking. With Lexi, some of the pain eased. It never left—it just abated a little. He needed this time away with her, this time out from his memories.

"Adam?" Her hand was on his shoulder, a soft, tentative touch.

"Yeah?"

"You need to come out here, don't you?" Her voice, it was so gentle, so caring.

"What do you mean?" Shit, she must have picked up on his thoughts. He'd become too pensive.

"It's your escape. Your reprieve from something."

He didn't answer, didn't want to.

"You've got that look in your eyes."

He lifted his glass, tried to take another sip, but he couldn't drink, couldn't swallow. He put the glass down. "What look?" He stared out at the night, heard the stream below trickling over rocks in its path.

"That haunted look." She dropped her hand from his shoulder to his arm and stood closer to him. "The one that tells me you've lived through the worst life has to offer." She touched his cheek.

Damn it. He couldn't get into this, not now. This weekend was meant to help him escape his memories, not confront them.

"What happened to you, Adam?"

He shook his head, found it impossible to speak.

"Talk to me, please."

The words jammed in his throat. He wasn't ready. He'd never be ready.

"Let me in, Adam. Help me to understand you."

If anyone would understand, it was Lexi. Part of him wanted to tell her, to open up. Another part couldn't go there. It hurt too damn much.

"Trust me," she whispered.

He shook his head again. "It's not a matter of trust."

"Then what is it?"

"Please, don't ask."

"I want to help you."

"It's too hard. I can't go there." Even he could hear the pain in his voice.

"Adam..."

"You have to cut me some slack on this one. Give me some space." He didn't mean to snap, dammit, it was the pain. He had to make it go away.

Her hand fell away and she took a step back. "I'm sorry. It's really none of my business."

Shit, now she was upset. He had to justify his actions. "Some things..." He cleared his throat, tried again. "Some things are just too...difficult to explain." Ah, crap. That wasn't it at all. "They're too hard to talk about," he corrected. Then for lack of ability to say any more, he simply repeated himself. "Some things are just too hard."

"Adam." She took his hand, held it. "I'm sorry. It really isn't my business, and you don't have to say anything." She opened her mouth again, shut it and chewed on her lower lip. Then, as if rethinking her words, she said to him, "You remember one thing. When...if...you ever need to talk, I'll be here, Adam Riley. I'll be right here."

Chapter Twelve

Lexi wasn't sure what woke her. Her eyes blinked open. For a few seconds, she couldn't work out where she was. The room was pitch black, the bed hard and unfamiliar, and a woodsy scent permeated the air. A cicada chirped outside and a frog croaked. She forced herself awake, waited for the fog to lift, and then she remembered.

She was with Adam, in his cabin. In his bed.

So, what had woken her?

A muffled sound, like a soft cough, echoed through the house. She rolled over, reached for Adam. He wasn't there. The sound grew louder. A painful, drawn-in breath followed by a moan had her sitting bolt upright. Then came the sobbing, like cries wrenched from a tortured soul.

She threw off the covers and slipped out of bed. Holding her hands in front of her, she made her way in silence through the inky blackness. The tormented cries guided her down the passage and into the lounge.

It wasn't quite so dark in there—a full moon shone through the open windows, bathing the room in pale light. Adam lay on his back on the couch. One hand was raised above his head, the other arm flung out over the edge of the cushion. Tears fell uninterrupted down his cheeks, and his face was contorted in an agonized mask. Harsh, barking sobs jarred the stillness around him.

Lexi's stomach clenched and she bit on her fist. Tears filled her own eyes and she watched helplessly as once again, Adam endured his unspeakable grief alone.

"Adam?" she whispered but received no response. "Adam?" She edged nearer, crouched before him on the carpet. "Riley?" He didn't move. She peered closely at him and realized with a start that he was asleep. "Oh, Adam," she breathed, her heart close to breaking. She took his hand, cradled it in hers and let him cry. Her own tears spilled over and she wiped at her cheeks.

Time passed, how much Lexi wasn't sure. Slowly, the distressed sobbing subsided. His cries became more subdued, turned into soft and steady weeping.

Careful not to wake him, she retrieved a roll of toilet paper from the bathroom and used it to blot his tears. The knot in her stomach eased as his weeping gradually diminished, leaving only the ragged breaths that rattled his body.

"Timmy," he moaned. Another tear slid unchecked down his face.

Hurt radiated from his sleeping form and pulled at Lexi's heart. He looked lost and alone and terribly, terribly sad. She perched beside him on the couch and cupped his cheek in her palm. "Hush now," she whispered as his chest shuddered in the aftermath of his grief. "Hush."

Moments later his breathing evened out. His pulse slowed down and his body relaxed beneath her arm. Just when she assumed he'd fallen back into a deep sleep, he gripped her elbow and gasped, "Timmy?"

"No, Adam," she said gently, not wanting to startle him, "it's Lexi."

"Lexi? What are you doing here?" He pushed himself up and stared at her, his eyes drawn in confusion.

"You were dreaming," she told him, keeping her voice low. "You...called out. I came to see if you were okay."

"Timmy." His shoulders slumped and his eyes closed. "I was dreaming about Timmy."

"You said his name a few times."

He nodded, keeping his eyes shut. "Did I say anything else?"

"No." She hesitated, then added, "You were crying."

His eyes opened and he stared blindly in front of him. "I always cry when I dream about him."

Again, her insides contorted at his pain. "Do you want to talk about it?"

He shook his head. His face looked pallid and bruised.

"Is there anything I can get you?"

"No, thank you. I'm okay now. It's over."

"Some water, maybe?"

"Nothing." He shook his head again.

She sat quietly, wanting more than anything to console him but unsure how to. "Adam, come back to bed. You need sleep."

He dragged a hand over his eyes. "I can't sleep. Not after the dreams. The memories won't rest."

What memories?

It didn't matter. All that mattered was giving Adam the comfort he so desperately needed. "Would it help if I held you?"

He looked at her, let her see his pain. "I don't know, sweetheart. But I'd sure as hell like to try."

CR

Adam awoke to the unfamiliar heat of warm, naked flesh. She lay spooned against him, her butt cradled in his hips, her legs pressed against his. The silky skin of her back was positioned so close his heartbeat ricocheted off her spine. Weak light peeked in from beneath the blinds, dappling the room with its dim rays.

He was already hard, bursting with a staggering need to shift her slightly and push into her moist depths. He craved release, anything to burn off the agitation left over from the night before.

He'd had one of his dreams.

Timmy called to him, crying. Adam couldn't find him. He searched, frantically, opened door after door after door. Panic set in. Dread squeezed at his throat so he couldn't breathe. Timmy was close. His cries pierced the air, wrenching Adam's soul—but he couldn't reach him. He yelled his name but his screams were mute. He sprinted in the direction of the cries but his legs didn't move. He tried. By God, he tried. Nothing was more important than finding Timmy, than helping him. Sweat poured from his forehead. He had to help Timmy. He had to find him. He had to, but he couldn't. He couldn't find him. He couldn't help him. He couldn't.

God help him, he couldn't find Timmy.

Awake, Adam could still hear the cries echoing through his heart. He clung to them helplessly until, like Timmy, they too slipped out of his reach.

Adam took a shuddering breath and grasped the only thing that provided him with any measure of comfort. Lexi.

He ran his hand down her side and over her hip, pausing at her thigh, absorbing its heat. He need only push gently on her leg to gain access to sweet relief.

She'd come to him, consoled him while he wept. Protected him while he slept.

His fingers trailed back up over her hip, across her arm and touched a bare breast. He swallowed hard, stunned by the intensity of his need for her. It wasn't just relief he sought. It was Lexi. He wanted her—and not just for a quick fuck. He wanted to make love to her, wanted the comfort and the passion only she could give him.

She stirred and stretched, then cuddled back into him. Goosebumps rose over her skin and she shivered. Her wakefulness did not end Adam's slow exploration of her body. He continued to stroke her, gleaning whatever pleasure and reassurance he could take.

She was silent but a wealth of unspoken words lay around them, covering them like a blanket.

"Morning," he whispered.

"Good morning," she answered but did not turn around.

Lord knew he appreciated it. He couldn't look her in the eyes yet, couldn't bear the sympathy he knew he'd find in her probing gaze.

Hot sparks ignited in his stomach as she arched into him. Her buttocks pushed against his erection and she sighed as he ground his cock into her.

He had to say something. It wasn't fair to put the onus on her to speak first. He knew she'd have questions, lots of them, but she'd be cautious about asking. When she'd tried yesterday, he'd told her to back off.

After last night, he couldn't avoid the truth any longer.

"You came to me." His voice was raw.

"You needed me," she replied simply but her body tensed,

as though she wanted to say more but held back.

He still needed her. As hard as it was to acknowledge, it was the truth. "No one's seen me cry in a very long time," he admitted hesitantly.

She took his hand and placed it on her breast, over her racing heart. "It must get lonely. Having no one to comfort you when you hurt."

Excruciatingly lonely. Nighttime was the worst, especially after one of his dreams. "I wasn't alone last night. You were with me." Usually he couldn't sleep afterwards. He'd spend the rest of the long, dark night prowling his house. Last night, he'd tossed and turned for a while but eventually, under her soft touch and soothing embrace, he'd drifted off to sleep.

She made a small sound in the back of her throat as he flicked his thumb over her pebbled nipple. A lick of desire shot through him.

"I'm glad I was there." Her voice caught and she cleared her throat. "Did...did it help?"

He dropped his hand to her stomach, brushed it over her belly, and she quivered.

Pain cut through him as he answered. "Nothing helps. But I was glad you were here." No one had held him after one of his dreams before. No one had been there to share his pain. He hadn't let anyone near. Until Lexi.

Adam inched his hand lower until he raked the hair on her mound, making her shudder. "I'm still glad you're here." He touched her clit and she gasped.

She opened her legs slightly so he could circle her swollen nub. Sensation coiled through him, settling in his rigid shaft.

"Adam...I—"

"Shh."

It was a delay tactic. She'd see straight through it but he didn't care. She was awake and she was responsive and he needed to come. They could talk later. He dipped his hand downwards, pressed ever so lightly, and she responded with a gush of warmth between her thighs.

"Aah," he breathed.

"Please," she whispered, "talk to me."

He dipped his finger inside, slipped it in through her warm, welcoming honey. "I want you, Lexi." Slowly, languorously, he withdrew and then slipped back in again.

She writhed against him. "You can't ignore me forever. I won't let you."

He pressed his thumb against her clit. "Do you call this ignoring you?"

She gasped. "You can't disregard what happened."

"We'll talk, sweetheart," he promised. "Later." When he'd had more time to distance himself from the dream.

She groaned as he pressed a little more firmly and ventured a little deeper.

"I need you, Lexi." He shouldn't admit it. He should just shut the hell up but he couldn't. He worked his hand over her, seducing her. "I never meant to need you..." He shook his head, dumbfounded by both the realization and the fact that he was telling her. "Somehow...it happened." How? When?

She started to say something but he cut her off. "Lean forward, very slightly." He couldn't hold back any longer.

She did and yelped as the action pushed harder against her clit.

"Don't move," he whispered. It took mere seconds to find a condom. Then he was back, cradling her, touching, probing her moist folds. He nudged her lips apart and sheathed himself deep inside her.

She cried his name out loud.

"Christ, Lexi," he gasped. "I need you."

He set the pace, plunging slowly in and out. She met him stroke for stroke, her breath coming in soft pants. He was very nearly mindless with desire. He trailed his hand down her back, found her buttocks and traced her cleft. She whimpered at his touch. Then he palmed both buttocks, pulled them apart slightly and thrust even deeper.

"Dear God... Adam."

The depth of emotion she wrung from him was confounding. He had to tell her, had to let her know. "You make me feel again."

She moaned and squeezed her inner muscles around him, sucking him into a vortex of pleasure. He spiraled off on a physical high. She pushed her hips back, met him time and again as he plunged ever deeper.

He couldn't get enough, wanted more, wanted all of her. "I thought...I would...never...want to...feel again." He spoke his words in time to the rhythm of his thrusts. "You changed that."

The tension built. His desire increased tenfold. He thrust a little faster as she tortured him with the wild gyration of her hips, and he knew he couldn't hold out much longer.

He twisted inside her, pulled out, plunged in and then did it again.

"Ohmegod. Adam, I...oh...oh, Adam." He twisted again and she exploded, juices of pleasure streaming from her.

Her orgasm threw him over the edge. He plunged into her one last time and lost whatever control he'd possessed. "Lexi," he cried as he exploded inside her, the gratification of his release more powerful than he'd ever anticipated. "Christ, sweetheart, I need you so bad!"

CR

Time passed and neither of them moved. Whether it was a minute or an hour, Lexi wasn't sure. They hadn't changed positions; he still lay behind her, keeping his face hidden. The longer they lay without speaking, the louder the silence became.

It wasn't just the two of them anymore. Adam's ghost sat between them.

When she could bear the tension no more, she asked him the question she knew he dreaded. "Adam, who's Timmy?"

His breath was ragged and an eternity passed before he finally answered. "He's my son."

Her heart stopped beating. "You have a son?"

"Had," he corrected, his voice a million miles away. "He's dead."

"Oh, Adam." She tried to turn around but his arm pinned her down. "When?" she asked instead.

"Ten years ago."

A decade and his pain had not yet relented. "How?" She already knew the answer.

He exhaled. "Cancer."

Lexi closed her eyes as they filled with tears. "How old was he?"

"Three. And a half." An iron clamp squeezed her heart. "He had a brain tumor."

Slowly his story unfolded. In a strained voice, Adam gave her the details. She understood how much the effort cost him. His arm and chest were rigid, his voice stoic. Quietly, she lay with him, desperate to console yet unable to intrude while he recounted his past.

"At first the doctors diagnosed epilepsy because he had seizures." His fist clenched and unclenched beside her belly. "So they put him on medication for it. Then they blamed all his other symptoms on the drug, like the nausea and the vomiting and the fact that he was so tired all the time." Clench. Unclench. "He started getting headaches." His voice caught. "They were so bad. Sometimes he'd just hold his head and cry." He swallowed. "We gave him painkillers, strong stuff. They didn't always help." Breath shuddered from his lungs. "We couldn't help him. I...I couldn't make the hurt go away. Sometimes, he wouldn't even let me hold him, he'd push me away and lie on the floor and sob in agony."

Tears ran down Lexi's face unchecked.

"Within a month, he lost coordination and had trouble walking. He'd fall over for no reason. The neurologist insisted on doing a scan, an MRI, and that's when they found it. They operated immediately—it was our only option. Can you imagine? He was only three and they took him into surgery and opened him up and cut into his brain." He took a deep breath and kept speaking. "It was too late. By then the tumor was so big and had grown into places they couldn't reach, and they couldn't get it all." He was silent for a long time. "He died eight weeks later."

His heart hammered against her shoulder and the muscle shifted in his arm as he clenched his fist again. "He changed. In eight weeks. Lost his words." He began to shake. "He'd try to say something but he wouldn't be able to find the right words, and he'd get so angry." He stopped, breathed, and started again. "There were the times he'd talk and look at us and wait for an answer. We couldn't respond, because...because, he'd spoken gibberish and we couldn't understand him."

155

He drew another shuddering breath. "He had nightmares, even when he was awake. He'd scream and scream, and no matter what we did, we couldn't comfort him.

"The end... Christ, it came so quickly. He couldn't walk or talk. He...he didn't even recognize us. There was nothing left of him. And then...and then...he...died." Adam's voice trailed off, his words reverberated through the early morning stillness.

This time when Lexi turned to him, he offered no resistance. She wrapped her arms around his shivering body and held on tight, fearful that if she let go, the hurt would overwhelm him and she'd lose him to his memories. He clutched her to him, and for the longest time the two of them lay in each other's arms. Neither said a thing. Words were unnecessary.

Hours later, they sat together in the kitchen, pretending to eat breakfast. Adam chased a piece of toast around his plate with a fork while Lexi picked at a grape, wondering how to phrase her next question.

"Where's Timmy's mother?" she asked finally.

"In Perth," he answered and stabbed the toast.

"Is she...are you married?" She had to know.

He looked up sharply, and then shook his head. "Divorced."

"Do you see her often?"

"I haven't seen her in years, can't face her. It's just too hard." His face was white. "I bumped into her in Melbourne last week." He lifted his fork, stared at the toast. "I didn't want to talk to her but I couldn't very well walk away, could I?"

"Did it end badly?"

He dropped the fork and gave up the pretence of interest in

food. "Not really. After Timmy died, Tracey and I drifted apart. We liked each other well enough. We simply weren't in love anymore. A dead child wasn't enough to carry a dying relationship."

Unable to sit any longer, he stood and paced around the room. "God, we were so young, so inexperienced. We couldn't give each other the kind of support we needed. She turned to her family and friends, I turned to mine and we forgot to be there for each other. It wasn't a nasty breakup. Just a kind of sad recognition that we couldn't be together any more. Not without Timmy." He stopped, stared out the window. "Our lives changed after that. I came to Sydney. She remarried. I think she's happy again. She has two kids now."

There was so much unspoken emotion in his voice. "Have you met them?"

He turned to face her. "Timmy's brothers?" His smile was lifeless. "I'm not strong enough for that. What if they look like him?" He shook his head. "What if I resent them because they lived and Timmy didn't?"

Her heart squeezed in her chest. He carried around so much pain. Had he ever worked through his loss? Or did he only acknowledge it at night, when sleep anaesthetized the grief?

"What about you, Adam? What about your life and your happiness? Don't you want to get married again, have more children?"

He looked like she'd punched him in the gut. "How could I ever have another child? Timmy was...was my life." His fist hit the wall with a resounding blow. "He died. I loved him, and he died. I can't do it again. Won't." He took a deep breath and then another, rubbed his fist with his other hand. "I can't even be around small kids, can't talk about them, not without thinking

157

about Timmy." His face hardened. "A wife and kids are not in my future."

That told her, didn't it? Lexi tried not to respond to his exclamation. It wasn't easy. Every minute she spent in his company, she became more convinced Adam was the man for her. How could she ever convince him of that?

"I'm happy where I am now," he concluded.

Happy? He was possibly the loneliest man she'd ever met. He wore his isolation like a life vest. While it kept him buoyant and alive, it also kept him adrift in a sea of people, not allowing him to ever reach out and grab onto another person's hand.

"Are you really? Happy, I mean?"

"Happiness is relative. Compared to ten years ago, I'm happy."

"And compared to eleven years ago?" She didn't need to add before Timmy got sick.

"That's an unfair question," he rasped.

"I'm just trying to understand you." His pain was palpable. "Oh, Adam, from where I stand, you don't look happy. You look hurt and alone and badly in need of a little loving."

"Maybe I am." He shrugged warily. "Maybe that's why I needed you here with me this weekend." His head dropped back against the window and his eyes closed.

"Do you feel better when I'm with you?"

"When you're with me, I feel. Period. It's something I haven't allowed myself to do in a long time." He didn't open his eyes. "That night in Melbourne, I felt more alive than I have in the past ten years. I...I liked it."

The vise around her heart loosened and she experienced a buzz of unexpected hope.

"Thing is," he continued, "I haven't allowed myself emotion

for such a long time, I'm not sure what do with it."

She stood and walked over to him. Wrapping her arms around his waist, she lay her head on his shoulder and held on to him. "You don't have do anything with it," she said. "Just feel. Just let the emotions be, accept them. You don't have to deal with them or act on them. If you're sad, cry. If you're happy, smile. Don't repress what's happening between us in case you get hurt again. Grieve over Timmy, but don't stop living, Adam."

His arms, which had been hanging loose at his sides, crept up and he clung to her, burying himself in her embrace. She held him, soothed away his pain, gave him her strength and willed him to be happy again, to feel again. As his resistance weakened and his muscles relaxed, she acknowledged to herself that he wasn't the only one going through emotional upheaval. Her own emotions were running amok.

She was falling in love with Adam Riley.

Problem was, she seriously doubted he'd ever allow himself the freedom of returning her love.

Chapter Thirteen

"You sure you're up to this?" Lexi paused just outside the restaurant.

He smiled. "I think I can handle it."

She bit her lip, uncertain. "They're gonna ask questions, you understand?" If she could've cancelled the dinner plans, she would have.

"We'll answer them."

She wasn't convinced. "They're persistent." Damn persistent. Leona had insisted she come tonight.

He laughed out loud. "We'll do fine."

"You don't mind?"

"I don't mind."

"Well...okay then. I suppose."

"Lexi, it's dinner, not the Spanish Inquisition."

It might as well have been. Lexi was a bundle of nerves. She hadn't told Daniel about Adam. What would she have said? *Oh, by the way, I accidentally slept with your friend a few weeks ago?* She hadn't told Leona either, for the same reason. *Lee— remember how I said I didn't meet Mr. Riley at the conference? Well...actually...*

There'd be a deluge of questions at dinner. How would she deal with them? Should she just come out with it and tell them all she'd fallen crazy, head-over-heels in love with him? Tell them that their spontaneous weekend away had been so incredible she had no choice? Tell them that Adam had bared his soul to her and she'd given him hers in return? Probably not. She'd probably need to tell Adam all of that first.

Maybe she'd just keep quiet and see where the conversation led.

"Come on then," she said, resigned to her fate. "Let me introduce you. Don't say I didn't warn you."

Daniel stood as they reached the table and shook Adam's hand. "Lex, AJ. Good to see you." He looked at Lexi with a raised eyebrow before introducing Adam to Amy, Leona and her partner, Annie.

Amy smiled at him. "I remember you from our wedding. Is that where you and Lexi met?"

"No. We met in Melbourne, actually."

"You did?" Leona shot Lexi a surprised look.

"Well, uh, we kind of bumped into each other there. I tripped and AJ caught me before I fell on my face. I just didn't know he was the man I'd been looking for."

Amy's eyes danced. "All your life?"

"No." She shot her sister-in-law the evil eye. "Just for the last six weeks."

Amy bit her lips and tried unsuccessfully not to smile.

"Why were you looking for him?" Daniel asked.

"She wanted money," Leona supplied helpfully.

"For what?" Annie asked.

"The sibling program."

The four of them nodded in understanding.

"So," Amy thought aloud. "You'd been looking for a man

you'd never met before to ask him for money."

"That sounds like my sister," Daniel said. "She's not shy, is she?"

Adam's smile was unmistakable. She just knew he was picturing her naked on the trunk of his car, diddling herself. "No," he agreed, "she's not shy at all."

Heat crept into her cheeks.

"I hope she asked nicely," Leona said to Adam. "She's been known to shoot her mouth off."

"Yeah, I noticed that about her," Adam said as he pulled a chair out for Lexi. "To her credit, she did ask nicely. Very nicely indeed."

"Should I just leave the table so you can talk about me in private?" Lexi asked.

"No need," Daniel assured her, "we can talk just as easily with you here."

Lexi humphed and sat beside Amy.

"So, AJ, how did she convince you to give her the money?" Leona wanted to know.

Adam took the seat on Lexi's other side. "Let's just say she knew which strings to pull to get me to agree." Under cover of the tablecloth, away from inquisitive eyes, he placed his hand on her thigh, reminding her of the strings they'd discussed in his office.

As if she needed reminding.

"Yeah, she's good at that," Daniel commiserated. "Talked me into doing the exhibition in about two minutes flat."

"Hey, don't complain," Lexi warned Daniel as Adam massaged her just above the knee. "The exhibition was a great opportunity for your career."

Daniel looked at Amy. "I'm not complaining. The exhibition

was a great opportunity, period." The two of them shared an intimate, sexy smile.

The same kind of smile that Lexi and Adam had shared at sunset in the mountains. He was thinking of it too. She knew because he squeezed her thigh gently and smiled at her.

"Were you at the exhibition, AJ?" Annie asked.

"I was. But not for long."

"Long enough to buy a few photos," Daniel said.

Amy leaned in close and without disrupting the conversation, said softly to Lexi, "He's hot."

"I know." Hot with a capital H.

"I watched the two of you at the wedding."

"You did? Why?"

"You were arguing."

"You noticed that?"

"Sparks flew all over the place, Lex. It was hard not to notice."

Shit. So much for trying to be discreet.

"From where I stood, I figured the argument would end one of two ways. You were either gonna kill him or sleep with him." Amy grinned. "My money was on the latter."

"Your money?"

"Yeah. Dan and I discussed it on honeymoon. We took a bet."

"You took a bet," she repeated, a little stunned. Her brother and sister-in-law had not only discussed her and Adam, they'd taken a bet about them.

Daniel leaned over his wife and whispered, "I bet you'd kill him. I had ten bucks riding on it."

Lexi shook her head in wonder. "You had nothing better to

do on your honeymoon than make wagers on my sex life?"

Daniel grinned. "Oh, we found a minute or two to do other things."

"Hey what are you being so secretive about over there?" Leona asked.

"Amy and Daniel were just telling me how they...struggled to find anything constructive to do on their honeymoon," Lexi answered.

"Oh yeah," Annie said with a laugh, "there's a real dilemma for you."

"Where did you go?" Adam asked as he brushed his hand along Lexi's thigh.

"Hayman Island," Daniel answered

Lexi couldn't suppress the delicious shiver that danced across her leg.

"I believe it's beautiful there," Adam said.

"Paradise," Amy agreed.

Paradise was right under the table.

"Do you have any pictures?" Adam dragged his thumb dangerously close to the juncture of her legs.

"Not one," Daniel said. "Amy wouldn't let me bring my camera."

Good grief, he wasn't going to touch her here, in public, was he?

"Hey," Amy said, "if you'd brought it along I wouldn't have seen you the entire time. I had to protect my...interests."

Lexi breathed a sigh of relief—or regret, she wasn't entirely sure—as Adam's hand slid back to her knee.

"Trust me," Daniel told Amy, "I only ever had your best interests at heart."

Leona whistled. "I just bet you did."

As everyone laughed, Amy leaned in close again and whispered to Lexi, "So, did I win?"

"Wouldn't you love to know," Lexi whispered back. If Amy pushed the tablecloth aside right now, she'd have her answer. She swallowed a low moan as Adam tickled her inner thigh.

"I know already. You've got the look of a woman who's been good and truly—"

"Oy. That's enough," Lexi cut her off with a snort. The only reason she had that look was because Adam's hand was sending thrills racing through her belly. "What are you being so nosy for anyway?"

"Call it payback." Amy smiled sweetly.

"For what?"

"Attacking Daniel with a cricket bat."

"What?" Lexi shrieked.

Conversation around the table ceased. Even Adam's hand stilled.

"You attacked Daniel with your cricket bat. Remember?"

"Well, bloody hell. I did no such...oh..." Lexi's voice trailed off. Oh. Whoops. How could she deny it?

"You did what?" Adam asked, shocked.

"Beat up my husband," Amy supplied helpfully.

"You weren't married," Lexi argued.

"Yet," Daniel added.

"What do you mean 'yet'? If I hadn't...hadn't told Amy I'd attacked you, you still wouldn't be married."

"My point exactly," Amy said with a self-satisfied smile. "You butt in. I butt in."

"Butt in? You needed me. Hell, someone had to knock a bit

165

of sense into you."

"So you hit Daniel with a cricket bat?" Adam asked, sounding mildly dazed.

"No," Lexi denied. Christ, at this rate he'd wind up thinking she was an axe murderer or something. "I didn't. I just, um, kind of told Amy I did."

"What for?"

"He made me do it." She pointed at Daniel, who sat grinning at all of them.

Adam looked at Daniel. "You did?"

"Didn't have a choice really," Daniel said.

"Why not?"

"Because I wasn't interested in him," Amy said.

"So Lexi had to beat Daniel up to get you to like him?"

"Pretty much," Daniel said.

"It was all a cleverly master-minded plan," Amy explained. "Daniel thought I took his friendship for granted. He wanted to shake me up a bit, get me to see I couldn't live without him."

"Which you can't," Daniel added.

"He got Lexi to phone and tell me he'd...um...accidentally been attacked. Needless to say, I nearly passed out from shock and had to race right over to see if he was okay."

"Yeah, and to nurse me back to health."

"And the rest, as they say, is history." Amy smiled.

"So you're saying you couldn't have gotten together without Lexi's help?" Adam asked.

"Or Leona's," Amy added.

"Leona?"

"Yeah," Leona said. "Danno thought a little jealousy was a good thing, so he and Lexi cooked up some story about me wanting to jump his bones. Thought it would make Amy jealous of me."

"It did," Daniel interjected with a triumphant smile.

"Yeah. Until I found out the truth."

"That the only bones Leona wants to jump..." Adam's eyes rested on Annie.

"Are mine," Annie said with a grin.

"I didn't find out that little tidbit until much later," Amy said.

"I had to tell her the truth eventually," Daniel said.

"Actually," Annie said with a mysterious smile, "you weren't the one who told Amy about us."

"What?" Daniel looked stunned.

Amy studied her nails.

"She found out quite independently of you," Leona added.

"She did?" Lexi demanded. She hadn't known that.

"Yes. She read it in our case file," Annie said.

"What file?" Lexi asked.

"The one at her clinic," Annie answered.

"What clinic?" Adam asked.

"Amy's a fertility counselor," Lexi told him. "She works at the IVF clinic here in the Eastern Suburbs." It suddenly hit her. She gaped at Leona. "You're not?"

It was Leona and Annie's turn to smile intimately. "We are."

No wonder Leona had insisted on dinner tonight.

"You are what?" Daniel asked them, and then turned to Amy. "And why didn't you tell me you knew about Leona and Annie all along?"

Amy shrugged. "Patient confidentiality."

"Patient confid... Oh my God." It was Daniel's turn to gape.

"We're going to be parents," Leona said with a twinkle in her eye. "Annie's pregnant."

The table erupted in chaos.

They were well into their main course before the oohing and aahing died down and Lexi noticed that Adam was more subdued than he'd been at the beginning of the evening. It was her turn to place her hand on his leg.

"You okay?" she asked softly.

"Fine," he answered.

"You're very quiet."

"Don't have much to say."

Of course he didn't. His thoughts were on Timmy. "The baby talk getting to you?"

He was saved from having to answer by a waiter clearing their plates away.

"We don't have to stay, you know?" Lexi said.

"Dessert's on its way."

"We can get it to go."

"It's a special evening. We can't leave yet."

"You sure you're up to this?"

"Positive."

"You're a nice man, AJ Riley."

"Adam," he corrected.

"You're a nice man, Adam."

A few minutes later, Lexi paused with her spoon mid-air. Adam's gaze burned her. The heat in his eyes made her breath catch.

"Is it good?" he asked, motioning to the spoon. The crème

brûlée hung suspended between them.

"Very," she answered. All she could think was how much better it would taste eaten off his naked stomach. With a shaky hand, she put the spoon in her mouth.

He watched her, his pupils dilating. "Looks delicious." His voice was low and a little hoarse.

The creamy custard slid down her throat, sweet and smooth and satisfying. "It is."

"You have..." he touched her lower lip, "...a drop, just here." He wiped it off and then brought his finger to his mouth.

Her own lips parted as he licked off the cream. Christ, he was right. The dessert looked delicious.

Their eyes caught and locked and the rest of the room disappeared.

03

He clamped his hand over hers, stopping her from opening the door. "If you don't want me to stay the night, tell me now," Adam growled in her ear. "Because once I step foot in your unit, you are mine." This wasn't like him. Usually he didn't need anyone. Since the weekend, since he'd spilled his guts to her, he seemed to need her more than ever.

"You're going to Hong Kong tomorrow, Adam. Of course I want you to stay the night."

Damn it, he didn't want to go overseas. Not now. But perhaps it was better; perhaps he needed to put a little distance between them—before he did something really dumb, like fall for her.

"Besides." She smiled at him, flashing her sexy dimples. "I got the dessert to go after all." She let them into the apartment.

"A single helping wasn't enough?" He could probably force a spoon or two down—after he'd had his way with her.

"Let's just say..." she paused and her eyes flickered to his groin, "...I wasn't overly fond of the way it was served."

His pulse jolted to a jerky gallop. "What, you didn't like the plates?"

"The plates were fine," she said. Her lips looked luscious, inviting. "I just thought the crème brûlée would taste better if I licked it off you."

The blood in his veins emptied into his groin. He was hooked. The more he saw of her, the more he wanted her. Was it the fact that she was whole, healthy? That she'd been through shit and she'd dealt with it, come out a better person for it? Unlike him?

Or was it the fact that she was hot and as turned on by him as he was by her? What had compelled him to confide in her about Timmy? How come he didn't regret it? He'd wanted her to know. Wanted her to share his pain.

He hadn't wanted to share his pain in a long time.

She was too far away; he pulled her to him, taking her mouth in a hot, steamy kiss. He tasted the sugary sweetness of the dessert on her tongue and the erotic promise of sex on her lips.

She was more than welcome to lick the dessert off him. Hell, she could suck it, bite it, nibble it or just plain eat until she'd had her fill. He tugged her shirt over her shoulders and made short work of her bra. She could eat whatever the hell she liked off him. After that, he was going to make love to her. He was going to bury himself deep in her tight, wet center and fuck her. Just like he had yesterday and the day before that. Just like he intended to do as soon as he got back from this business trip.

"Christ, you're beautiful," he rasped as he stripped off her low-cut pants and left her standing in nothing but a white, lacy thong. He shed his shirt without conscious thought.

His hands were on his zipper when she said, "Wait. Let me do it."

Another dart of desire speared through him as she placed her hand where his had been a moment before and caressed him. She didn't need to touch him. Just being with her was the biggest aphrodisiac of all.

The rasping movement of the zipper drove him damn near insane and he was ready for dessert long before she'd knelt down and drawn his jeans over his hips. He kicked off his shoes and the pants followed.

"Adam," she murmured before touching her lips to his abdomen.

His stomach muscles clenched involuntarily under her lips and she moaned. Her warm breath caressed his belly button and then floated lower until faint puffs of air whispered over his cock. It twitched and grew, straining against his undies.

This was more than just sex. Whatever was transpiring between them was real and it scared the crap out of him. If it were anyone else, he'd hit the road.

Nothing could keep him away from Lexi.

Over the weekend she hadn't just given him physical release. He'd expressed and experienced emotions he hadn't acknowledged in years. He'd shared Timmy with her.

He'd given her his son.

Lexi inched the confining material over his bulging member, freeing him. He could almost feel her mouth closing around him, taking his whole length in. He wanted those hot lips wrapped around him, sucking him dry.

"Follow me," she said and stood.

"Where are we going?" He could hardly walk in this state.

"Not far." She pointed to one of the armchairs in the lounge room. "Food tastes so much better when you're sitting, don't you think?"

She was in the mood to play. His own mood lightened even as his need intensified.

She snagged a bag from near the front door and flicked on a lamp in the lounge. Light flooded the room. "I like to see what I'm eating," she told him.

"I like to watch you eat," he said and sat. He was barely aware of the pillowed seat beneath his ass—such was his anticipation. He'd watch her as she ate up every inch of his dick. If watching her eat dessert in the restaurant was any indication, watching her blow him would be staggering.

She pulled a small plastic tub from the bag and showed him. "Dessert," she said and opened it, dipping her finger inside.

When she lifted it up again, it was covered in the creamy custard. He watched as she proceeded to treat her finger to exactly the same indulgence he'd fantasized about. She wrapped her lips around it and sucked it dry. His breathing shallowed as he struggled to stay seated. The need to haul her closer and push her head down into his lap was overpowering.

She dipped back into the tub and then traced his mouth. Instinctively, he licked his lips, tasting the rich, sticky substance she'd left behind.

"Uh uh," she warned. "No sharing." She straddled him so her groin rubbed enticingly on his upper thighs. "I have to make this little tub last a long time."

She lowered her head to his and starting with his upper lip, systematically licked off every drop of custard. Then she moved onto his lower lip to do the same, pausing to nibble here and suck there. When the outside of his mouth was clean, she dipped her tongue between his lips and kissed him, sharing her mouth, allowing him the tiniest sample of dessert. It was not the crème brûlée that had him desperate to taste more, but the salacious heat of her mouth.

His nipple tightened reflexively as something cold touched it. Lexi massaged it with her hand, rubbing custard into his skin. She released his mouth and lowered her head to taste the rigid nub. The gentle scrape of her teeth against the sensitive flesh, the hot licks of her tongue, were almost too much, the pleasure almost painful.

"Dessert taste any better?" he asked, struggling to form the words. His hands tangled in her hair, tugging on the silky strands as she worked her magic.

"A little," she conceded before subjecting his other nipple to the same treatment.

If it weren't for the promise of her mouth on his cock, he'd lift her up and slide her back down until he was sheathed in her body. But Adam was too selfish to hurry this exercise along. He intended to enjoy every second of it. Besides, if she sat on his dick now it would be game over.

She drew gooey lines down his stomach and climbed off him to kneel between his legs. The muscles in his gut clenched and unclenched in time with her tongue as she lapped up the sticky mess.

"It tastes better," she said as she dabbed at the last drop of cream on his belly. "But there's still something missing." She dipped into the dessert again. "Something hard." With her free hand, she cupped his balls and he nearly hit the roof as she stroked them. "And salty." She nibbled on her lower lip.

"Something a lot more satisfying than dessert." She slathered the crème over his cock, making good and sure to cover every visible spot of skin.

The contrast of the chilled cream under her warm skin had him squirming in his seat. How would he feel in the hot, wet cavern of her mouth?

Electrifying.

Her greedy mouth was everywhere, voraciously lapping up the dessert, licking him clean, sucking at the more difficult spots. Supper had clearly not satisfied her appetite; she devoured him with a fierce hunger.

He forced oxygen into his air-depleted lungs. Good God, where had she learned to do that? Her carnal tongue wrenched a groan from deep in his gut. The pressure built. His balls tightened.

She massaged them lightly, erotically, as her mouth consumed him.

"Lexi. Christ, sweetheart...stop!"

She sucked a little harder, took him in a little deeper.

"Lexi, Jesus..." It was too much. He couldn't stop. Not now. He exploded, pumping semen into her mouth.

She stilled as he came, waiting until he'd spent every last drop. When he finished, she looked him dead in the eye, and with her mouth still wrapped around him, swallowed the whole damn lot.

He collapsed against the back of his chair, winded.

What the hell? He should be soft, should be utterly spent. He wasn't. Not by a long shot. Lexi ran her tongue up the length of his cock and he shuddered, oversensitized to every miniscule touch. She grazed her teeth over his tip.

"Lexi," he groaned, dazed by her renewed assault.

Adrenalin coursed through him. His cock, semi-erect after he came, roared back to life. A strangled groan escaped him and he stilled her head with his hands. "I can't," he growled.

"Oh, believe me," she said as she rose. "You can and you will."

He was putty in her hands. She was right. He could and he would. Especially after watching her remove her panties. He caught a glimpse of her naked hips, saw her glisten with a cream more scrumptious than any dessert.

He was falling for her. It was the only explanation. He couldn't be this aroused, this soon, if it was just sex.

She leaned forward, kissed him again. Her mouth was sticky—with custard and come, a mixture of sugar and salt, and he groaned as he tasted her. He reached out, stroked her moist folds, touched the cream that coated them, drank in the soft moan that she emitted.

It had never been just sex with Lexi. Even their first time had been too intense, too amazing to be just sex. It was more. Way, way more.

His fingers were wet when he withdrew them and he pulled his lips away from hers, breaking the kiss. He traced her mouth and when he kissed her again, the taste of her desire combined with his own and with the dessert left him rock hard and rearing to go.

"You see," Lexi said as she straddled him again. "You can." This time when she settled down, she impaled herself on him.

Adam swore out loud as her hot core enveloped him.

He wasn't falling for her. He'd already fallen. Hard.

Her hair was wild, the curls tousled in every direction, and her eyes were glazed. He surged upwards, thrusting into her, and watched in satisfaction as she arched her spine and dropped her neck backward.

She wound her arms around his neck and clenched her inner muscles around him, gyrating her hips, taking him deeper, then releasing him and easing up slightly.

Christ. She was heaven wrapped around him. She rocked above him and he lost himself to her rhythm. Nothing could feel better than this, nothing could feel sweeter. This was the wonder of making love.

Even the bad stuff didn't seem so bad when Lexi kissed him.

Her back arched, her breasts jutted out and he dipped his head and kissed them. He laved her nipples, licking and sucking on them until she moaned mindlessly in his lap. Her movements became frenzied, less controlled, her inner muscles pulled at him and she began to tremble.

The quivering reverberated all the way through to his bones. It was the shiver of a needy woman, a woman who'd clamped down on her own pleasure too long and now demanded release.

He'd give it to her. He'd give her anything. Everything.

She twisted slightly and leaned forward, changing the angle of penetration. Adam nearly lost it. He grabbed her hips and held her still. Too late—the process had begun. Powerless to stop, he surged upward and she moaned his name as he drove deeper into her.

This was not just sex.

Her lips mashed against his balls, enhancing the sensation tenfold. Again and again, he thrust, again and again, she moaned, until her trembling turned to violent shaking and her muscles clamped down around him and she came.

Not ten minutes before, he'd exploded in her mouth. Now,

still not quite believing himself capable, he exploded again. Stream after stream of come pulsed into her as torrents of pleasure and emotion assailed him.

This was what making love was all about.

Chapter Fourteen

The hot water ran over her shoulders, washing away the soapy residue. Behind her, Adam's hands worked their magic as he lathered more soap onto her back, massaging her pleasantly stiff muscles.

"Mmm. That's good," she purred, keeping her eyes closed.

"Very good," he agreed as he slid his slippery hands around her ribs and cupped her breasts.

She leaned back into him and he nuzzled her cheek. "Did you enjoy tonight?" she asked.

He chuckled in her ear. "As if you even need to ask."

Lexi smiled the smile of a well-satisfied woman. "I meant this evening. The dinner. Did you have a good time?"

He ran his hands hypnotically over her stomach. "It was nice. They're a good crowd."

"They liked you too," she said.

"They did?" he asked, sounding surprised.

"Yep. Told me so when you went to the bathroom. They managed to squeeze it in between the four million questions about you and me."

His hands stilled. "What did you tell them?"

"Not much," she answered. "I just said you were a nice guy and the only man who'd ever given me nine orgasms in one night."

He snorted in her ear. "You didn't."

"Course I didn't. Even though you are the only man who's ever given me nine orgasms in one night." She turned in his arms and they shared a long, wet kiss, drawing apart only when the water pulsating over them ran tepid.

Adam switched off the taps and climbed out of the shower. He held a towel open for her, wrapped her in it and then proceeded to dry himself. Lexi watched the muscles in his arms and shoulders ripple dramatically as he rubbed his towel over his hair in quick, hard strokes. A shaft of desire stabbed through her. They'd made love not thirty minutes ago and still she wanted him.

"I know the evening couldn't have been easy for you," she said carefully. "All that talk about babies. Jesus, even I thought about Timmy. I can only imagine what went on in your head."

He dried a little faster. "It's not my favorite topic of conversation."

"That's why you were so quiet," Lexi said.

He nodded. "That and the fact that it was a special time for Leona and Annie. They didn't need my two cents' worth. They're happy. It wasn't my place to cast a shadow over their telling." He wrapped his towel around his waist and turned around.

Their eyes met in the mirror and her heart began to pound. God, she loved him. Goddamn it, she wished he could love her back. She knew that until he resolved his issues about his son, he'd never allow himself that luxury. He simply did not have the capacity to give himself a little happiness, not while he still grieved for Timmy. "Do you think the pain will ever ease up?"

He shrugged. "I'd like to be able to reach a point when I can

179

think about Timmy and smile. Remember all the good times. I just haven't reached it yet."

"Adam." She bit her lip, thinking how to word her question. "Have you...did you ever mourn Timmy after he died?"

His eyes turned hard. "I mourn him every day of my life."

"I know you do. I can see it. Your wounds are still raw ten years later." No wonder he'd appeared so cold the first time he'd met her. He used distance as a means of covering up his trauma. If no one could get close, no one could see his terrible injuries. "You never allowed yourself a chance to heal, did you?"

"Heal. You expect me to heal after what happened?" His tone was harsh.

"I don't expect anything. I..." Shit, she had to tread carefully here. "I just wish you were free of your guilt of living."

"So what are you saying?" His eyes grew cold. "That I should be glad that I lived and Timmy died?"

"Adam," she gasped. "You know I'm not saying that."

For a moment, he dropped his defenses and his shoulders sagged. "Do you have any idea how many times I've wished our roles had been reversed? How many times I wished I were the one who'd been sick, who'd died, and not Timmy? Do you have even the slightest idea?"

He straightened his shoulders, stood a little taller, and his voice picked up volume. "Do you know what it's like to watch your child die? To live through your child's death? Do you?" He turned around, grabbed her shoulders. "Do you know how hard it is not to mourn, not to spend every minute of your life reliving the last minutes of your son's? I don't think you do. I don't think you have a fucking clue."

His anger was so intense it was almost tangible. How much of it had he kept buried inside all this time, festering?

"I don't think anyone has a fucking clue. You want me to live guilt free? Yeah? Well how fucking easy do you think that is? Should I just pretend it never happened? Just move on and get another life, have another kid? Is that what you want from me?"

She understood his rage—she dealt with it every day at work, with patients who'd lost children to cancer. Only Adam wasn't work, he was personal. His anger affected her. With clients, she kept her distance and her objectivity. With Adam, she couldn't. His pain was too real to her. She wanted to share it with him, wanted to identify with his emotions.

"I want you to be happy again, Adam. The only way you can do that is by mourning your son. You have to feel the pain to get through it. Allow the hurt in, deal with it, accept it. Maybe then you'll be able to find a place for happiness too."

"You think I don't let the pain in?"

"I think you do. All the time. You just don't express it. You keep it bottled up so tight that the only time it comes out is when you're asleep and you have no control over it."

A muscle twitched in his jaw and his mouth clenched shut.

She tucked her towel around her breasts and stepped forward. "Let go, Adam. Let your emotions out. You want to feel again, you said so in the mountains."

"Oh, it's that simple, is it?" he asked savagely. "I should just let myself cry for a few days and then I'll be fine. I'll be the old Adam all over again. Not a worry in the world."

"No." Lexi shook her head. "I don't think you could ever be the old Adam again. You've been through too much, experienced too much to ever be the same. Timmy's illness changed you. To expect yourself to go back to what you were before is naïve and unrealistic. To expect to experience joy again is not. It will just be different, because you're different." She touched his arm. "Let go of Timmy. Let yourself mourn him properly so you can say goodbye. So you can start to live again."

"What if I don't want to live, not without him?"

"I think you do." She took a deep breath. "I think you do because you're with me now. Something is telling you it's time to try again. To give life another shot."

"Fuck that, I don't deserve another shot."

"What? You think you don't deserve to be happy?"

"No. I think I don't deserve to be with you." His voice lost its life. "I tried to be with a woman once. I failed. Miserably. Our son died."

"Your son didn't die because of you."

"I couldn't help him."

"No one could. It doesn't mean it was your fault."

"I was his father."

"Yeah, but you weren't God. What happened to Timmy was out of your hands. That doesn't mean you have to punish yourself. Tracey was his mother and she couldn't help him either. She understood that."

Adam nodded. "She's happy again."

"You can be too."

"I want to be." He dropped his head. "I want to be happy again, it's just that the thought of moving on, it's too—" He stopped mid-sentence and the color drained from his face.

"Adam, what's wrong?"

He smacked his forehead. "For fuck sake. How could I have been so stupid?"

"I...I don't understand." His face was white and his eyes had turned to ice crystals. Naked fury danced in their depth.

"Us. You and me. Careless, negligent, stupid." He swore

again.

"What are you talking about?" Lexi grabbed his arm and shook it. The sudden change in his demeanor scared her.

He took a snarling breath and hissed out, "Protection. We didn't use any fucking protection tonight." He hit the basin with a curled-up fist. "The condoms are still in my wallet."

Horror washed through her. They'd made love and neither of them had given a second thought to condoms. She gaped at him, speechless.

"You know my position on children. Damn it, an unwanted pregnancy's the last thing I need now."

It wasn't exactly on top of her list of priorities either. One day, yes—but not now. "Adam—"

"This is a fucking catastrophe. I'm a damn fool. Shit, I was so horny tonight, so turned on, I completely forgot." He swiped a hand through his damp hair. "This is a problem, Lexi, this is a very big problem."

Who was he kidding? His little swimmers could be hastily making their way to her fertile ovaries right this minute. Who the hell knew? One of them might have struck it lucky already.

She blanched at the thought.

Adam stalked out of the bathroom and into the living room. She darted after him. He snatched his clothes up from the floor, shoved his legs into his pants and pulled them up.

"Wait, what are you doing?"

"What do you think I'm doing?" He shot her a scathing look. "I have to go."

"You're leaving?" she squeaked. "Now?" In the middle of everything? Okay, he was angry, but they needed to discuss this. Leaving wouldn't resolve anything.

"Another thing you forgot?" he asked acidly. "I'm going

overseas tomorrow."

Forgot? Hardly. She dreaded tomorrow, dreaded the thought of two weeks without him. "Adam, you can't go yet." Panic clawed at her chest. "We should talk, work this out before you leave."

"Talk?" he roared. "You think talking will stop you falling pregnant?" He did up his belt. "I have to pack."

Oh, and packing was a more effective means of prophylactics? She gawked at him in disbelief. It would be so easy to throw her sarcasm in his face, to haul insults back at him, but one of them had to remain level-headed and Adam wasn't exactly volunteering for the job. "Please, think calmly for a minute. We can't just assume this...mistake will result in a pregnancy. In fact, it's most unlikely." At least she prayed it was unlikely. "But just in case, we have to work out how we'd deal with it if I were."

Adam froze, but just for a second, then he pushed his arm into a shirt sleeve. "This is all I need. Two weeks overseas wondering whether the hell you're pregnant or not." He pushed his other arm into his shirt. "Goddamn it. How could I be such an ass? So hot to get into your pants, I couldn't think logically for one minute. Couldn't act like a man and put a condom on."

Lexi couldn't repress her snort. Oh, he'd acted like a man earlier. Now he acted like a boy.

He shot her a nasty look. "Think this is funny? You're as much to blame as I am. You could also have used your head a little."

She bristled at the cruelty in his tone, tried unsuccessfully to ignore it. Their discussion had brought down his defenses—she mustn't forget that. She'd pushed him on issues he might not have been ready to tackle. He was vulnerable and hurting.

Still, it didn't give him the right to act like an animal—or to treat her like one—no matter what the circumstances. "Are you saying it's alright for you to get carried away by the heat of the moment, but not me?" Her spine bristled. Shit, remaining even-tempered wasn't so easy. At the best of times, Lexi had trouble controlling her tongue. A potentially explosive dilemma like this one didn't help at all.

"No. I think we both made a huge mistake tonight." He grimaced. "You knew my thoughts about babies. What the fuck do you think we just discussed? I told you I don't want to have more kids." His voice turned hoarse but no less angry. "I told you about Timmy and you didn't remind me to use protection."

Timmy. Her breath caught in her throat. That was a low blow. It was bloody unfair of him to use his son to make his point. A point she already knew and understood all too well. How could she defend herself against a dead child?

She didn't want to try.

"Don't do it," she warned, her own temper seconds away from erupting. "Don't try and use your son against me. Yes, you told me about him and about your refusal to have more kids." Pain flashed across his face but was quickly masked by fury and loathing. "Timmy has nothing to do with what happened between us tonight."

"What happened tonight was the action of two careless, stupid adults..." Adam's eyes narrowed to dangerous slits and his lips thinned in fury. "Unless..."

Prickles of apprehension tapped on her spine. "Unless what?"

A muscle ticked in his jaw. "Unless only I was careless, and you did this on purpose."

"Pardon?" She *had not* heard him correctly.

"You did, didn't you?"

"I did what?" she asked, aghast. No way could he think that.

"You did this on purpose."

Lexi's jaw dropped open. He did. He honestly believed she'd tried to get pregnant. The prickles of apprehension turned to stabbings of rage.

"What did you want, Lexi?" he seethed. "To trap me? You knew I couldn't make a commitment to you. Did you think you'd just try and get one anyway?"

Lexi stared at him, too stricken to answer. The very thought had bile rising in her throat. Was he out of his mind? Was the man deranged?

"You think it would be that simple? You'd get pregnant and I'd suddenly want to be with you forever? Is that what all the talk was about? I should get over Timmy so I could accept another child into my life. A child that was a mistake? A set-up?"

Her chin hit the floor as the impact of his accusation hit home.

How dare he? They'd shared too much for him to believe that of her. Sure, he was angry and vulnerable, but even in that state he couldn't think so little of her. Could he?

"Sorry, lady, it doesn't work that way. You don't stoop so low and get away with it."

Lexi pulled back her hand to slap him, then stopped herself. Fury bubbled in her belly. She'd likely break his nose if she hit him now. As enticing as the thought was, it was not very practical. It would just compound the whole screwed-up situation. Not only would he think she'd tricked and deceived him, he'd probably sue her for damages too.

"I expected more from you, Lexi." He tackled the buttons on

his shirt. "Way more."

She curled her hand into a fist next to her leg and reminded herself that blood was hard as the devil to clean up.

"I never thought you'd stoop to such levels," he ranted. "I told you how much I could give. You didn't listen."

Why, the arrogant son of a bitch. Lawsuits and bloodstains be damned.

Her hand landed with a resounding crack on his cheek. She kept it well clear of his nose and watched in satisfaction as a dark red impression of her hand formed just below his cheekbone.

For once, Adam was speechless. He looked from her hand to her face and did not say a word. For a couple of seconds, astonished disbelief replaced the anger in his eyes.

"You think I planned this?" Lexi took advantage of his silence to have her say. "You think I want to get pregnant—or open myself up to the prospect of a sexually transmitted disease?"

His face was ice cold. "I assure you, you won't get a sexually transmitted disease from me. Can you give me the same assurances? Can you assure me you won't get pregnant?"

"Fuck you, Riley." She couldn't possibly give him that guarantee and he knew it. "You know what? I was right about you from the beginning. You're a cold, callous bastard. A heartless, cruel, vindictive bastard." She glared at him. "How dare you make such unfair assumptions about my behavior? How dare you take our night of beautiful lovemaking and turn it into some cheap scam on my part?"

His glared back at her, but before he could speak, she beat him to it. "Yes, we're facing a crisis. Yes, I may well be pregnant, but accusing me of such treachery is not a solution to our predicament." Goddamn it. They had to face it together, come up with a plan that suited both of them. "I know you don't want children, Adam. I get that. It doesn't reduce my risk of pregnancy now."

They'd come so far together. They'd made real progress. Why did he have to cut it all short? Push her away again? Damn, he didn't just push, he picked her up and threw her. Was she too close? Had she scared him? Made him see how lonely he really was? Was his only means of defense to attack?

Logic told her it wasn't personal. Adam was angry and hurt and he took it out on her. Her clients did it all the time. Only Adam wasn't her client. He *was* personal. He'd hurt her. Pissed her off. No one pissed her off and got away with it. No one. Not even the man she loved, and not even under dire circumstances like these.

"You know what?" she asked, her voice a venomous whisper. "I tried. I really tried to like you. For a while there, I did. I started to care, even fell a little in love with you." A little? That was a laugh. There wasn't a cell in her body that didn't love him completely—even if she detested him right now. "And what did it get me? Nothing, apart from your contempt and your accusations. Well, guess what? I'm through trying. I've had enough. I will not stand here and allow you to abuse me like this." She stalked to the front door, pausing only to pick up his shoes and socks. Then she yanked the door open and threw them out.

"Leave, please," she told him dispassionately, though her stomach and heart yelled for him to stay. To top it all, her head reeled at the prospect of facing a possible pregnancy alone. "Get out of my home and out of my life, and this time—don't come back."

He stared at her for a minute, his face grim and set. Then he gave a short, sharp nod, fastened his pants and walked out the door. He didn't even give her a backward glance as he leaned down and picked up his shoes.

Lexi's temper ignited. The asshole could at least have tried one more time. Could have turned around and apologized. Could have begged her forgiveness. Could have promised he'd stick by her if she was pregnant. Could just have said goodbye. He could have, but he didn't. He just walked out, and she lost it.

Before she could stop herself, she called after his retreating form, "How does it feel, Riley? To think that I may be pregnant with your child, and to know that you will never find out—one way or the other?"

Lexi collapsed against the front door, aghast. Had that really just happened? Had Adam accused her of trying to trap him with an unwanted pregnancy?

She didn't know which was worse—the prospect that she may be pregnant or the weight of his accusation. Nausea, which had threatened to engulf her for the last ten minutes, seized control.

She made it to the bathroom in the nick of time. The contents of her stomach emptied themselves into the toilet bowl. She threw up twice before the bile began to settle.

This was not how she'd perceived her future. This was not the white-picket-fence happy ending she'd always dreamed about. She existed in a nightmarish world of bad mistakes. The first bad mistake had been Adam. The second had been forgetting the condom.

Now she faced her third bad mistake alone—the possibility of a pregnancy with a child whose father despised her.

Chapter Fifteen

Adam was in hell. No two ways about it.

He swore and rubbed his hands over his eyes as he sat up in bed. His shoulders ached and his neck was in spasm. Every time he tried to turn it to the left, sharp jabs of heat tore through his shoulder, straight up to his chin. Christ, he was barely awake and he had a tension headache. Another one.

The hotel bed was not to blame. It was perfectly comfortable. No, the headache had nothing to do with the current five star accommodations and everything to do with the hellcat whose home he had stalked out of the previous night. Or was it the night before? He'd lost track of time.

He checked his watch. Six forty-five in the morning. Which meant it was eight forty-five back home. He reached for the phone and for the umpteenth time since he'd landed in Hong Kong, punched in the code for Australia, and then Lexi's mobile number. For the umpteenth time, he got her voice mail. He swore, not bothering to leave a message.

Next, he dialed the hospital.

"Department of Social Work, this is Penny speaking."

"Lexi Tanner, please." If he couldn't get her at home, he'd get her at the office.

"One moment please and I'll connect you. Whom may I say is calling?"

"Adam Riley."

"Oh, um. AJ Riley?"

"Yes, AJ Riley."

"I'm sorry, Mr. Riley, Lexi is not taking calls at the moment."

"You just said you'd connect me."

"I know, but Lexi's signaling to me that she's not accepting calls."

"She's there?" *Thank God.* "Let me talk to her."

"Uh, she's not available now. Would you like to leave a message?"

"No. I want to talk to her. Put her on."

"I'll try." There was a moment of silence and then Penny said again, "I do apologize for the delay. Lexi can't speak right now. If you leave a number, she'll get back to you."

Yeah, right. "Never mind. I'll try again later."

He heard Penny sigh over the phone. "You can try. I'm just not sure you'll have any luck."

Adam swore silently. "Thank you for your help," he said before hanging up.

Fuck it.

He threw off the covers and went to shower. She wasn't going to answer. Not if he phoned every day, five times a day, for the next two weeks.

The spray of water did nothing to relieve his mood and the soap did not wash away his remorse. His disposition only worsened when a knock sounded on the hotel door.

"What?" he snapped.

"It's me. Open up."

Adam clamped down on his irritation and let Matt into the room.

"We leave in thirty minutes. Thought you might want to grab a bite first," his friend said by way of greeting.

Adam checked his watch. Even if there were time, it was pointless phoning her again. She wouldn't answer. He nodded at Matt and grabbed his briefcase. "Let's go."

Brodie followed him out of the room. "You going to talk about it?"

He pursed his lips. "About what?"

"About whatever the hell it is that's bothering you." Of course. Matt had to say something sooner or later.

Rather than riding in the elevator, they chose the stairs. Adam took them two at a time. "Nothing's bothering me." That should cut the conversation short.

"Cool," Matt said amiably. "And by 'nothing', I assume you're referring to Lexi Tanner."

Okay—maybe not quite as short as he'd figured.

"Do you know when last I saw you this bent out of shape?" Matt asked. "Ten years ago."

The vigorous walk downstairs didn't seem to affect Matt. His own breathing, however, was substantially heavier than usual. "You remember how I behaved ten years ago?"

Matt stopped Adam at the entry to the dining room. "Mate, you were fucked up. You couldn't sit still. You couldn't look me in the eye. You couldn't smile. Same as now."

Christ, not Matt too? Was the whole world conspiring to make him relive the last few months of Timmy's life? Tough, he wasn't going there again. He refused. He turned to his friend and forced his mouth into a tight smile. Anything to get the conversation back into the present. "Better?"

Matt grimaced. "Damn, don't do that. You look like you just swallowed your own fart."

This time, Adam's grin was genuine, although he shook his head at Matt's description.

"Better," Matt approved. "Now tell me. What's up?"

He suppressed a sigh. "I'm fine, mate. Nothing's wrong."

"You can feed the rest of the world that crap. I know you."

"Don't you ever mind your own business?" As if he needed to ask.

"Nope," Matt confirmed as a waitress led them to a table. He had the grace to wait until they'd both helped themselves to food from the buffet before resuming his line of questioning. "What happened with Lexi?"

"Nothing," Adam told him flatly. "It's over." Strange his voice could sound so even when his gut was tied up in knots.

Matt's nod was full of sympathy. "You fucked it up."

"Christ, give it a rest." He knew he'd fucked it up. He didn't need Matt rubbing it in.

"I can't, and you know why? Lexi is the right woman for you. You're an idiot to let her get away."

Adam raised his eyebrow. He was an idiot all right, no denying that. As for letting Lexi get away...well, it wasn't his choice anymore. She'd tossed him out on his ass—and he'd deserved it.

"I've been working with her for over a month," Matt said. "I've gotten to know her a little. She's the one, mate. You and I both know it."

Adam ate his toast in silence. Matt's words were immaterial. Lexi detested him and he couldn't blame her. He'd been a complete prick—or should he say bastard?

"Does she know about Timmy?" There was none of Matt's usual caustic humor in the question. Only a ton of empathy.

He chewed methodically, swallowed and stared at his plate. "Yes."

Matt's gaze burned his forehead. "Fix it."

He glanced at his friend. "Fix what?"

"Whatever you did to screw up your chance with her." His eyes blazed. "Fix it."

Adam shook his head. If he could take back what he'd said, what he'd accused her of, he would. In a heartbeat. "It's too late."

"You want this, mate," Matt said. "You told her about your son."

He stared at Matt for a long moment. Everything had changed. The stakes were different. It wasn't just about him and Lexi anymore. There was a pregnancy to consider now.

He shuddered. *A child.*

"Fight for her, Riley."

An unborn baby.

"She's worth it," Matt insisted.

Fear gripped his spine. *Lexi and his baby.*

"Mate." Matt's voice was sharp, snapping his attention back to the table. "She's the right woman for you."

He knew what he had to do. He'd known for a while now. Not that he wanted to, not on any level. Hell, he'd rather gouge his eyes out with a fork. There wasn't a choice. If he didn't act now, there'd be no way he could ever sort out this whole fucked-up scenario.

With hands as cold as ice, he reached in his briefcase for

his mobile phone.

"You phoning her?"

Adam almost laughed out loud. He shook his head. "Travel agent. Change in plans, Brodie. I won't be flying home with you when this trip is over."

CR

"You gonna tell me what's got you so pissed?" Daniel asked. "You've been a bitch for weeks now."

"I told you, I don't want to talk about it," Lexi snapped. She'd been mooching around the whole morning, wallowing in self pity.

"Yeah? Well, tough. Where's AJ?"

She looked up sharply. "What's he got to do with it?"

"You tell me." He unwrapped a chocolate-chip muffin, broke off a piece and set the rest on her desk between them. "I know he's been away. That the problem? You missing him?"

No. She wasn't missing Adam. She was positively pining for him—which only made hating him more difficult. Misery plagued her like an impenetrable cloud. She couldn't see through it, couldn't find a single thing in her life to take away her grief.

Even the sibling program, which was about to be launched and was running more smoothly then she'd ever dreamed possible, had lost its sparkle. She found it impossible to get excited about much when her heart had been wrenched in two.

On a rational level, she knew Adam wasn't the asshole he'd acted like that night. She recognized the real man behind the façade. The gentle, tender Adam, whose capacity for love knew no boundaries. The damaged Adam, who feared intimacy of any kind because he equated love with pain. He'd lost the person who meant more to him than anyone else. Years ago, he'd been free to love and to be loved. To lavish affection on those closest to him. His payment for that love had been death and divorce.

She knew his reaction to the condom issue had been an impulsive response to a situation that had the potential to increase his torment. She'd pushed him that night. Pushed him to a point of emotional helplessness. Perhaps, if he had not been so vulnerable at the exact moment he'd remembered the condoms, the situation would never have spiraled out of control.

Instead, Adam found himself in the very situation he'd never wanted to be in again, at a time when he had no defenses. He'd instinctively done the only thing he could to protect himself—he'd attacked.

She didn't condone his behavior, not by a long shot. On a rational level, though, she understood it. That didn't make anything about her response to his behavior rational.

Understanding it did not ease the pain he'd inflicted on her. Not one tiny bit. It didn't stop the tears or the ache or the emptiness inside. It didn't dampen her anger or lessen her incredulity at the way things had panned out. It also didn't give her false hope that their relationship stood any chance of succeeding.

Worst of all, it didn't help her love him any less—which made everything a million times more harrowing. Despite how she felt, she and Adam were history. They had no future together—he'd made that perfectly clear.

"It doesn't matter," she told her brother. "It's over."

"What's over?"

Duh! Men. How dense could they be? "We are. Him and me. Our relationship. Okay?"

Daniel looked astonished. "What happened?"

She took a piece of his muffin and stuffed it in her mouth. She didn't want to talk about it. It was too bloody painful. She chewed, swallowed, stared at the remaining muffin.

"Lex?"

"We had a major blow-out," she admitted reluctantly. "He walked out on me."

"He did?" Daniel frowned. "You guys looked pretty tight. I thought this was a sure thing."

"Yeah?" she snapped. "Well it wasn't."

"Lex, I'm not the enemy," Daniel reminded her quietly.

She couldn't help it. Her eyes filled with tears and she had to gulp down a lump in her throat. "I'm sorry, Dan." She knew it was unfair to take her aggression out on him. He wasn't the baddy. "I just feel pretty shitty right now."

He nodded. "Yeah, I can see that."

She sniffed and blinked back her tears.

"Tell me about the fight."

What could she say? She didn't want Daniel to know about the terrible deed Adam had accused her of.

"Lex? What happened?"

It hurt too much to remember. She shook her head.

"Lexi..."

He used his no-nonsense big-brother tone of voice. It was useless trying to sidestep him. If she got away from him now, he'd just turn up on her doorstep later to get the rest of the story.

She took a shaky breath. "We weren't really fighting at first. We were just talking." They were more than talking. They were breaking through some of the barriers Adam had wrapped

197

around himself. They were making progress.

"About?"

"It's not important." Yes, it was, but she wouldn't break Adam's confidentiality by telling Daniel. "Suffice it to say it was a sensitive subject."

"And?"

"And Adam was a little upset." She'd pushed him on issues that were deeply personal and deeply painful. "So was I." Much as she'd tried to remain calm, Adam's allegations had gone too far and she'd lost it, shot her mouth off in a truly spectacular fashion—perhaps her grandest performance to date.

"So you fought?"

If he called hauling out the heavy artillery and blowing apart their relationship fighting. "Yes, but not about the issues we were discussing."

"I don't understand. What did you fight about then?"

Her cheeks began to burn. How did she explain the finer points of all this to her brother? She could barely comprehend it herself. What would he say?

"He thinks I tried to trap him...by getting pregnant."

Daniel choked on his muffin.

It took several minutes before he recovered from his coughing fit. "Where the hell did he come up with an idea like that?" Daniel demanded when he was finally able to talk again. His face was red, his eyes watered and anger blazed off him in waves.

Lexi studied her nails. "Well... You know the night of Leona's dinner?" Dang, this was humiliating. She and Dan were close, sure, but sharing the intimate details of her sex life was a little too much information—even for siblings. "We, uh, kind of got carried away."

Her brother shifted in his seat. Apparently it was too much information for him as well. Then he grimaced. "You forgot to use protection."

"It was a mistake, Danno. I swear." Her face burned. Bile rose in her throat again. She had never—ever—deliberately forgotten to use a condom.

"Of course it was," he rushed to reassure her. "I don't doubt that for a second."

Tears rushed back to her eyes. At least someone believed her.

She pressed her lips together, determined not to cry over Adam anymore. How could she hate someone and love him at the same time? Love him so much she physically yearned to see him again? To touch him? To throw her arms around him, hold him and never let him go?

"Does this mean you're going to make me an uncle?"

"No," Lexi answered flatly. "I'm not pregnant."

A week after he'd stormed out of her unit, she'd gotten her period. Never, in all her years since puberty, had she celebrated the rites of womanhood like she had that day. Relief washed through her, leaving her limp as a dishrag. *She wasn't pregnant.* At least that was one less complication in the Adam saga.

He didn't know yet. If he did, would he care? Would she care if he cared? Yes, dammit, she would. That was her whole problem—she cared too much about what Adam thought.

A tear spilled out despite her previous determination not to cry. Then another and another.

Daniel watched silently as she wiped her eyes with the back of her hand. Then he asked the question only a brother could ask and survive to learn the answer. "Did you want to be?"

She gaped at him. "What kind of a question is that?"

"Lex, you're crying," he pointed out. "You started crying at the same time you told me you weren't pregnant. I just wondered."

She wasn't crying about not being pregnant, she was crying about Adam. Again. "No," she sighed. "I don't want to be pregnant now. Sometime in the future, yes, but only under the right circumstances. I want to be married and happy and excited about the prospect of a family." What she didn't want was to fall pregnant under a nasty haze of unfounded suspicion.

"Have you spoken to him since?"

"No." She shook her head and took a piece of muffin. She wasn't hungry, she just hoped it might distract her from her misery. Maybe the chocolate would make her happy.

"He doesn't know you're not pregnant?" Daniel raised an eyebrow.

"No." She decided against telling Dan the bit where she'd promised Adam he'd never find out. She ate the muffin instead.

"Don't you think he deserves to know?"

"No." That was the irrational part of her answering. The part that wanted him to suffer as much as she had.

Of course he needed to know. She was certain he was in all sorts of hell wondering if she'd conceived his child. She just wanted him to suffer a little before he found out.

She sighed. "Yes. I thought I'd wait 'til he got back before I told him."

"And when does he get back?"

She gave in to a sudden overwhelming need to inspect her nails. "Last week."

"What? He's been back a week and you haven't spoken to him?"

"He hasn't tried to contact me," she mumbled. Granted, he'd phoned her in the beginning. More than once. Still enraged at the time, she'd refused to speak to him. She'd even threatened to disembowel Penny with a pencil if she put any of his calls through to her. Since then, she hadn't heard from him. Not a visit, not a phone call, not a word. Not one word. Nothing.

"What does that have to do with anything?" Daniel shook his head in disbelief.

She swallowed, cleared her throat and swallowed again. "He doesn't want to see me. If he did, he would have tried to get in touch." Yep. The irrational Lexi again. The proud one who believed that if Adam wanted to see her, he would come to her. He hadn't. That could only mean he wasn't interested. He wasn't interested in her and he wasn't interested in her possible pregnancy.

"Hang about, mate," Daniel said. "He needs to know. Since when has someone not wanting to speak to you ever stopped you from going to see them anyway?"

"Since I'm in love with this someone," Lexi answered despondently.

Daniel didn't even pretend to be surprised by her confession. "All the more reason. What are you waiting for? Go and see him. Now."

"Now?" She couldn't hide the panic from her voice. *Not now.* It was too soon. She wasn't ready. She couldn't face him. "Dan, the media conference is tomorrow. I can't just leave the hospital. I have too much to do. The program opens in one week." It was far easier to hide behind work than to pluck up the courage to go to him.

"I thought Abbey had taken over the program?"

"How do you know Abbey?" Lexi asked, looking for any means of diversion. This was a good one. She had mentioned she'd hired someone. She hadn't told Daniel her name.

"I hang around the ward a lot. I get to hear things, meet people."

Of course he did. Ever since he'd done the shoot at POWS, he'd become a regular here. If there was news, Daniel knew it.

"Sexy little thing, isn't she?" her brother mused.

Good. He'd bought into the diversionary tactic. "You're not the only one who thinks so. Matt's commented a couple of times too."

"She doing all right at the job?"

"More than all right. She's brilliant. With her on board, the sibling program can't fail."

"You trust her?"

"Of course I do."

"Then she can manage without you for a while. Go and see him."

Bugger. She should have seen that one coming. Daniel had seen straight through her change in conversation. Now she had no excuse. All she had left to offer was the sad truth. "I don't know if I can, Dan. I don't think I have the guts."

"I'm sure Abbey will be just fine without you."

"I'm not talking about Abbey. I'm talking about me. I don't think I have the guts to face Adam." Her voice dropped to a whisper. "What if he really does hate me and honestly thinks I tried to trap him? What if he doesn't want to see me again?"

Daniel refused to play into her self-pity. "And what if he does, Lex?"

She couldn't give herself false hope. "Then he'd have phoned," she sulked.

"What are you," Daniel sneered, "sixteen again, waiting for the boy to phone you? Get over it, mate. If you want him, go and get him. Go tell him the news."

Lexi didn't budge. She wanted him—more than anything. Nevertheless, rejection was a heavy price to pay for taking a chance. She doodled on her desk pad.

"What are you waiting for?" Daniel asked.

"I—"

"Go." He stood, took the remainder of the muffin with him and yanked the pencil out of her hand. "Now."

"Okay, already." She rose too and muttered under her breath, "Bully."

"Maybe so." Daniel grinned at her. "At least I'm a married bully. Now go and clear things up with your man, Lex. I suspect he's waiting for you."

Chapter Sixteen

He wasn't.

According to Genevieve, he wasn't even in Sydney. His secretary didn't know where he was. He'd simply left a message for her to cancel all his appointments for a week.

Lexi went home. Okay, so maybe Adam hadn't contacted her because he wasn't back yet. The thought didn't stop her from sinking deeper into depression. They'd made such incredible progress before *that* night. They'd forged a bond she knew he'd never have dreamed possible. With a little more time she was convinced she could have broken down all of his barriers, given him reason to want a future again.

One mistake. One stupid, thoughtless blunder and everything was ruined.

She loved him—despite how much he'd hurt her. Despite the fact that he was a stubborn idiot and had developed defense mechanisms more effective than the Great Wall of China. They were made for each other—couldn't he see that? Why did he have to hide behind their terrible mistake, and in the process destroy any chance they might have had?

Lexi tried to look at their relationship from a different angle—anything to help her understand why things had gone so wrong.

Maybe she was mistaken. Maybe she hadn't gotten as close as she'd thought. Perhaps instead of breaking down his defenses, she'd only reinforced them. Perhaps by pushing him to face his past, she'd destroyed their chance at a future.

The doorbell rang, jarring her out of her thoughts. Shoot, she didn't want to see anyone. She wanted to wallow in self-pity alone, away from prying eyes. If she sat quietly and pretended not to be there, maybe whoever it was would go away.

The doorbell rang a second time, and then a third.

"Lexi?"

Oh, sweet Lord.

"Open up, I know you're in there."

His voice was muted by the door but she'd recognize it anywhere.

"Your car's outside, I know you're home."

Holy shit. He was here. He'd come to her. What would she do, what would she say? Would it be inappropriate to not say anything? To just grab him by the collar, haul him close and kiss him? To fuck him right there in the open doorway?

"You can't ignore me forever, Lexi."

What if she cried? What if the relief of seeing him again was too much and she lost it completely, started sobbing hysterically as soon as he walked through the door? What if...what if he was only here on business and he wasn't interested in seeing her personally, didn't want to know about the pregnancy?

"Open up!"

She did, although her hands shook so hard she had trouble with the lock.

"Hello, Lexi."

There he was. Adam Riley, on her doorstep.

Sweet Lord, he looked good. Better than she ever remembered. A little thinner, maybe, but still heart-stoppingly gorgeous. Those shoulders, those enormous shoulders. She wanted to throw herself between them so he could wrap his arms around her. So she could feel safe again, secure in the knowledge that he was back.

"We need to talk," Adam said quietly.

His voice ripped through her heart like a hurricane. Her ribs constricted, making breathing difficult.

"May I?" He gestured to come in.

She nodded and stepped wordlessly aside, suddenly terrified of what he would say. Of what she would say and how she would say it. Whatever happened, she needed to set things straight. Needed to get their relationship back on track. She had to do whatever it took to get him to stay. She loved him too much to let him leave again.

Suddenly the prospect of being pregnant with his child didn't seem so awful—not if it was the only way she could keep him in her life. Lexi dismissed the thought as soon as it popped into her head. Yes, she loved him, hungered for a future with him, but not enough to stoop to such levels of treachery. Nothing would ever make her stoop to such levels.

He sat on her couch, pausing only to place a brown paper bag on the coffee table.

Lexi numbly chose a chair opposite him, eyeing the bag cautiously. What was it? Her attention flicked from Adam to the parcel and then, because she couldn't keep her eyes off him, back to Adam. His beautiful face was expressionless. She couldn't read it, couldn't find a clue as to what the parcel might contain.

"Go ahead," he said. "Open it."

What the hell was it? A peace offering? A restraining order?

"It won't bite. I promise." Was that an attempt at a joke? She looked at him. No. No humor in his eyes, just a steady intensity that made her heart race.

Her silence hung around her. She hadn't said a word since he'd arrived, couldn't think of a single intelligible thing to say. Better than shooting her mouth off, she supposed, and saying something she'd regret later.

Her behavior was a little surprising—being that her usual modus operandi was to dive headfirst into whatever situation she was presented with.

This was different. Her future happiness rode on this meeting and she wouldn't blow it. Fate wouldn't be so kind as to call again and offer her another chance. Better to remain quiet until she found the appropriate words to tell him she wasn't pregnant, to convince him she'd never trap him.

While her head and heart spun crazily, her body danced to an unsteady beat, responding on base instinct to Adam's presence. Every nerve ending tingled. He was here, meters away, and the physical awareness sent goosebumps skittering over her skin.

The bag lay unopened between them until inquisitiveness got the better of her and she picked it up shakily and peaked inside.

Naturally.

A rational sentence finally formed in her head. "This isn't necessary," she told him, thinking it nothing less than a miracle that she could talk. Her tongue was glued to the roof of her mouth.

"Yes it is," he countered. "I'm a responsible man and I hold myself accountable for my actions."

Lexi gave him a hollow smile and tossed the package on the table. The pregnancy test spilled out. "I don't need it, Adam. I'm not pregnant."

"You're not?" He sat up straight. "How do you know?"

"Because," she told him, "I got my period."

"Oh." He shook his head. Frowned. "I...uh... Oh," he said again.

He sank back in his chair, silent, and she gave him a minute to digest the news. He'd spent three weeks wondering, and in a second he'd discovered the answer. He needed the time.

Inscrutable emotion filtered through his eyes as he stared past her. Finally, he nodded. "There is no baby."

Was it her imagination or did he seem disappointed?

"No, Adam, much to your relief, I'm sure, there is no baby." She put the test back in the bag and pushed it across the table. "You're free to leave now." She prayed to God he wouldn't. He'd come to her of his own volition—to take care of unfinished business. Now that the business was settled, what reason did he have to remain? "You've fulfilled your duty. You've got your answer. There really is no reason for you to be here any longer." She hesitated before adding, "Is there?"

Her insides danced wildly, nervous tremors taking over. Would he want to stay?

He looked up at her. "I'm a real bastard, aren't I?"

At least he hadn't stood. At least he wasn't headed for the door. She took a minute to contemplate his question. His demeanor was different somehow. He was different. She couldn't pin down exactly how. He just wasn't the same.

"You can be," she answered carefully, terrified she might scare him off with her honesty. He had acted like an asshole the other night—but then, he'd been provoked.

"My behavior was inexcusable."

She didn't contradict him. She couldn't have if she wanted to. Her heart hammered so loud it was impossible to hear her thoughts, never mind voice them.

"I know you would never do anything as deplorable as trap me with an unplanned pregnancy."

Oh, thank you, God. Thank you, thank you, thank you. She almost wept at his words. Any strength she had in her arms drained out through her hands, and her shoulders sagged at the reprieve he'd given her.

It took a ridiculous amount of effort but she managed to collect her wits about her and answer in a steady voice. "I'm glad you understand that." She wasn't ready to let her guard down. He'd hurt her deeply and a simple acknowledgement of her innocence wasn't enough.

"I was a complete prick and I apologize."

She should just accept his apology and end the conversation now. Sitting this close to him was too difficult. She wanted to touch him, wanted to tear his clothes off and mold herself to his naked body—but that was out of the question. It would be much wiser to just ask him to leave so she wouldn't have to endure the torment.

She couldn't ask. There were too many burning issues she needed resolved. Too many reasons she wanted him to stay.

"What would you have done, Adam? If I were pregnant?" Suddenly she was desperate to know.

He sighed. "Does it matter now?"

"Yes, it does." He hadn't just abandoned her. He'd come back to take responsibility. The question was, what kind of responsibility would he have taken? The responsibility of raising another child? Financial responsibility? Or the responsibility of ensuring she had a termination?

A muscle worked in his jaw. "Whatever needed doing."

"Uh uh. Too vague." She wanted specifics. "What would you have done?"

He sighed and stared behind her at a point on the wall she couldn't see.

"I went home," he said. "Back to Perth."

That wasn't an answer. "I'm not following you..."

"I haven't been back in almost ten years. Not since I filed for divorce."

If she'd thought she was good at diversionary tactics, Adam was obviously an expert. Despite herself, she was sucked into his narrative. He'd told her he couldn't stay in Perth after Timmy's death, told her he hated everything the city represented, and yet he'd gone there now. "I thought you were in Hong Kong."

"I was. I went to Perth afterwards. I just got back."

Which explained why he wasn't in Sydney this last week. "Why did you go?"

"Because of you. Because of me." He kept staring at the invisible point behind her back. She studied him silently, gave him space to gather his thoughts. Noticed again that he seemed different somehow. Less removed, maybe?

"I went to visit Timmy. To spend some time with..." He cleared his throat. "To spend some time at his grave, to speak to him a little."

"Oh my God." Stunned, she swallowed down an unexpected lump in her throat. After their argument, she never dreamed she'd hear him say that. Never thought for one second he'd face his past head-on. "You did?"

"I went to say goodbye." He finally looked at her. Where she expected to see heartache and pain, all she found was quiet calm. The haunted quality that usually shadowed his eyes was gone. "And to let go of my anger. You were right. I'd been holding on to it too tight."

She floundered, overwhelmed by his confession. "That couldn't have been easy." Her throat was all clogged up.

"It wasn't. It got ugly. You ever see a grown man cry?" His laugh was empty and trailed off as her answer hung silently between them. She'd seen *him* cry.

If he stayed here much longer, he'd see her cry. She was barely holding it together.

"I can't say I'm not sad anymore. I am. I always will be. I can't even say I've accepted Timmy's death. But I guess I'm coming to terms with it. Learning to live with it."

He'd done it. He'd taken a giant leap and faced his grief over Timmy's death. Dear God, that must have been impossible. It must have ripped his world apart. Nevertheless, he'd done it. He'd survived.

That's when she worked out what was different about him. He'd lost his edginess. The cold detachment was gone. Before her sat a man who was ready to participate in life again. Ready to live—and not just exist.

Would he want to include her in that new life? Please, *please,* let her be included.

The suspense drove her crazy. She was an emotional wreck, pretending to be objective when she was so crazy in love with him she could hardly see straight. Her stomach was a mass of wobbly jelly.

She couldn't let him see what he did to her. Not yet, not until he'd told her about Perth, about Timmy. "You seem different," she said instead, giving him an honest assessment. "It's almost as if you're less aloof, less angry with the world." Less angry with her.

"I am," he said. "Or at least I'm starting to be."

"You can't be healed overnight," she cautioned. Yes, he was different. Still, grief took a long time to overcome. She'd hate for him to have false expectations.

"I can't be happy overnight either. I can be happier. I am." He paused. "I went to see the boys."

"Tracey's sons?" Holy shit. He'd scaled mountains without her.

He nodded. "Timmy's brothers."

"Adam... Where did you find the courage?" His heart must have hammered when he'd been introduced. Adrenalin must have taken over, let him run on autopilot.

"It wasn't as bad as I'd thought it would be." His answer was a sharp contrast to her conjectures. "I guess I'd just built them up in my mind, made them into something they're not."

How'd he do that? Clear such an enormous hurdle without even touching the bar? What about his biggest fear? Had it come to bear? "Did they...did either of them look like Timmy?"

He shook his head. "Not really, no. Can you believe that? All this time that's what kept me away. There were definite similarities. Corey, the younger one, has the same quirky smile and behaves the way Timmy used to. That could be regular three-year-old behavior and not specific to brothers."

He was so okay with it, Lexi thought. So...unaffected.

"Jason has the same hair color but other than that, nothing. I think whatever else I recognized in them was more their resemblance to Tracey than anything." He shrugged. "They're good kids, both of them. But they're not Timmy."

"Did you...are you okay?" What an inadequate question. It didn't begin to cover everything he must have experienced.

"Actually, yeah. It was harder to drive to the house and ring the doorbell than it was to talk to them. The anticipation was far worse than the reality." He leaned forward, rested his hands on her table.

She found herself staring at his long, strong fingers, resisting the impulse to take them and hold on for dear life.

"It's a relief, you know, to realize I can be around kids again and not resent them for living when my child didn't. You were right. It wasn't anybody's fault that Timmy died. It was just something that happened. Something I couldn't prevent. Something no one could prevent." He looked into her eyes. "You helped me see that, and for that I am eternally grateful."

He'd done it because of her and because of their mistake. He'd done it because he'd thought she might be pregnant, and he needed to confront his past before he could deal with his present. He'd done it because, because... She couldn't continue her line of thought. He'd done it. That was all that was important.

And then he smiled at her, gave her one of those traffic-stopping smiles, and her heart crashed into her ribcage, which in turn smashed through any previous resolve to hold back until he'd finished speaking. The walls of the dam burst open and everything came tumbling out of her mouth. She couldn't stop the words. Didn't even try.

"I love you, Adam Riley. I don't care if you've sworn off ever loving again or you don't want a future with me. I love you. I love that you tried to let me into your life and I love that you came back when you thought I was pregnant—even though you don't want children." She started to cry. "I love how much you love your son and I love how hard you've tried to come to terms with his death."

She took a deep breath, tried to stem the tears and only cried harder. She cried for all his pain and she cried for Timmy.

She cried because she loved him and she cried because she'd been through three weeks of hell. She cried because although he'd come so far, she still didn't think he was capable of returning her love. Lastly, she cried because she couldn't help it.

"It's okay that you don't love me," she said between sobs, struggling to focus through her tears. "That you can't love me back. I'm just happy that you're willing to give your own life a second chance. I'm happy that you're ready to move on." She was happy for him. It didn't mean her heart wasn't shattering in her chest at the same time.

She was a mess. Her nose ran, her mascara left smudges on her hand when she swiped uselessly at her tears, and her skin had turned all blotchy. It always did when she cried. She didn't give a damn. She loved him and she wanted him to know.

"I know I should be sorry I pushed you so hard, made you confront Timmy's death. I'm not, because look at you. You're...you're getting better. You're happier. I can't be sorry for that. I won't be." She sniffed loudly. "Because I love you, and I want you to be happy." She sniffed again and then again, and then she ran out of steam. "Because I love you."

She had to give herself credit. When she let go, she really had her say. No holding back for Lexi Tanner. Maybe one day she'd learn to think before she spoke but today wasn't that day.

Adam probably thought she was a stark raving lunatic. *She* thought she was a bit of a lunatic. She grabbed some tissues from her pocket and blew her nose noisily. Then she blotted her eyes, took a deep breath and drew her shoulders straight.

"So." She looked at Adam, saw his bemused face properly for the first time since she'd started crying. "As I said before, I'm not pregnant. You're free of any responsibility. Thank you for buying the pregnancy test. As you can see, it's not necessary."

She stood and headed for the door. "Perhaps I'll see you at the press conference tomorrow?"

He stood up too and caught her wrist as she walked past him. With a single tug, he spun her around and pulled her in, and before she knew what had happened she was in his arms.

Then he kissed her.

They'd shared some incredible moments before. This went beyond anything Lexi ever imagined. His mouth took possession of hers and proceeded to short-circuit every nerve synapse in her body. He held himself flush against her and usurped her senses. Sounds no longer made sense. Colors blurred together and massed behind her eyelids in a dazzling explosion of light. She was weightless, held down only by the intensity of his kiss and the emotion pouring through him.

This moment wasn't about passion. It wasn't about need or lust or sex. It was about love, pure and simple. Adam loved her. He told her in the most effective way he knew how.

She kissed him forever. She kissed him until the sweet joy of love mingled with the salty tang of tears and she realized she was crying again.

She pulled away, wiped at her eyes and was stunned to find them dry.

"They're mine," Adam whispered hoarsely, and she stared at the wet tracks running down his cheeks.

"Oh, jeez, Adam, I'm sorry. I didn't mean to make you cry."

He smiled at her through his tears, flashed her the traffic stopper. "I would have asked you to marry me, you know."

"What?" Her mind was on mental overload. She was processing too much information at once. She thought he'd just said he would have married her.

"If you were pregnant. I planned on proposing."

He *had* said it. "Why?" she asked stupidly. "You don't want to have more children." She tried not to think about the cruel joke fate played on her. Dangling *forever with Adam* before her eyes and then snatching it away, all because she wasn't pregnant. How fucked up was that?

"Didn't," he corrected. "I didn't want more, until I was confronted with the possibility that you might be pregnant."

"I don't understand." Her brain still malfunctioned from his kiss. She couldn't think straight.

He took her hand. "You screwed with my perceptions of reality, sweetheart. You changed me."

"Are you telling me you want to be a father again?" Lexi would never use the word incredulous in everyday conversation. Right now that was the only word that could adequately describe her state of mind.

"Thinking you might be pregnant changed me. It made me sit up and seriously consider what it might be like to become a dad again. That's when I knew I had to go to Perth, had to put my past to rest." He lifted her arm, pressed a kiss on the inside of her wrist. "I'm not living in the past anymore. I'm living here, in the present, with you. In this reality, the biggest loss would be if I didn't have more children."

She gaped at him.

"In answer to your question, yes, Lexi, I want to be a father again, and more than that, I want to be a father to your children."

"Mine?" Damn, there went her ability to construct full sentences.

"Yes, yours." He frowned, clenched his jaw. "There's something you should know. Something I've spent three weeks coming to terms with." Guilt and remorse clouded his face. "That night, when we fought? I didn't just forget to use condoms. I think that subconsciously I chose not to."

She gawked in disbelief. "Pardon me?" He'd put her through hell, blamed her for their joint mistake, charged her with trapping him with an unwanted pregnancy—when all along he'd *chosen* not to use condoms?

His eyes filled with shame. "I'll understand if you hate me, my accusations against you were cruel and unfounded. If it makes you feel better, I didn't sleep for days afterwards. I lay in bed at night thinking about what happened and wondering why I'd claimed you tried to trap me, when I clearly knew it was untrue."

Oh, she didn't hate him. Not by a long shot. She loved him so much she thought she might burst from it. Still, his acknowledgement of her innocence went a long way to soothe her previous wrath.

He took her hand, held it in his. "It took a while to see things clearly. For so long I've looked at the world and at my life with jaundiced eyes. After ten years of convincing myself I never wanted to marry again, suddenly there you were. Suddenly, against my will and my beliefs, I wanted a future with you. Longed for a future with you."

He took a deep breath. "But I equated that need with betrayal. I believed that in order to be with you, I had to give up my past, give up Timmy." His voice caught. "I couldn't do it, Lexi. I couldn't betray him like that. He's my son." Tears shone in his eyes. "I wanted it. So damn much." He paused, swallowed. "I think in the end, my need for you overrode my common sense, overrode my distorted loyalty to Timmy. I think I must have subconsciously concluded that if I made you pregnant by mistake, I wouldn't have a choice in the matter. I'd have to marry you."

In a warped kind of a way, she was flattered. Working

within his own emotional limitations, he'd devised a plan to be with her. A pretty screwed-up plan, but an effective one nevertheless. Without giving up his guilt, he'd tried to work her into his future. He'd almost destroyed their relationship in the process but at least he'd tried.

"You're saying you tried to trap me by getting me pregnant?"

He gave her a half-smile. "Ironic, isn't it."

Heartbreakingly.

She didn't want him on those terms. She didn't want him to marry her because he had no choice. If she and Adam were ever to be together, it had to be because he loved her unconditionally—the same way she loved him. "It doesn't matter where your future leads you, Adam. Timmy will always be a part of it. He's a part of you."

"I know that now. I also know that I don't need to make excuses to be with you anymore. We can have a future because I want it, not because I don't have a choice."

Her chest constricted. Dare she hope? "Do...do you...want a future with me?"

"Christ, sweetheart, can't you see? I want it more than anything."

She released a breath she hadn't known she'd been holding. "Oh, thank God."

"You...you don't hate me for what I did to you?" The fear in his face touched her heart.

"I tried to," she admitted. "But I couldn't. I love you too much."

The sound he made as he crushed her in his arms was something between a cry of pain and a gasp of relief. "I love you, Lexi," he rasped in her ear. "I have since the night I saw you at

Daniel's exhibition. It's just taken a little time for me to realize it."

"Adam..." Her heart filled with a joy she hadn't believed possible.

"Marry me, Lexi."

She pulled back from his grasp and stared at him, amazed. An hour ago she didn't know where he was. She'd feared she might never see him again. Now he'd just proposed. "But I'm not pregnant," she said stupidly.

He laughed unsteadily. "We can change that, when you're ready. In the meantime, we can enjoy practicing."

He kissed her again then, soundly, and she lost herself in the dizzying array of emotion washing through her. He loved her. Enough to marry her and start a family.

The world spun, leaving her light-headed and giddy.

He loved her.

She smiled against his lips. Adam loved her and he wanted her to have his children. AJ Riley, who never wanted to have another child, wanted to have a family with her.

She'd done it. She'd broken through his barriers and reached his heart and, well, he loved her. Adam Riley loved her and she loved him too. Could the world be a better place?

"So will you?" he asked when he pulled away.

"Will I what?"

"Marry me?"

Lexi threw her head back and gave a loud whoop. "You just try and stop me, mate. You just try and stop me."

Chapter Seventeen

Lexi raced across the lobby of the building and pushed the button. Her patience ran low as she waited, her foot tapping an anxious beat. She was late. They'd arranged to meet five minutes ago and this wasn't exactly the kind of place she could keep him hanging around.

At last there was a ding and the lift arrived. The doors opened and she stepped inside.

It was full. People must have gotten on in the car park. She didn't care. She pushed the appropriate button and stared blindly at the numbers as the carriage made its way slowly up.

How she realized he was in the lift, she didn't know. She felt his presence as vividly as if he'd touched her. The hair on her neck stood on end and a slow tremor took over her body. Pivoting around, she looked past the faceless people behind her and found him at the back of the elevator.

Their eyes caught and held. The air was sucked out of the lift. He was there, so close and so unreachable, another face in a sea of people. Yet it seemed as though they were the only two in the confined space.

The bell dinged several times and their fellow travelers got out one by one or in small groups. Lexi gave no thought to them leaving. Her total conscious mind was focused on him.

Then there were two of them, two adults and the audible hum of awareness buzzing between them.

Lexi dragged her gaze away from his to focus on the control panel. She reached out, pressed *Emergency Stop*, and the lift ground to a halt.

"You're late," he accused.

"Sorry, couldn't be helped. I had to do something first." Her hands were already working on the buttons of her shirt.

"Do you have any idea how many trips I've had to take in this lift?"

"Do you have any idea how arbitrary they'll seem compared to the trip you're about to take?" She opened her blouse and her breasts spilled out, unobstructed.

He swallowed. "You're not wearing a bra."

"I'm not wearing panties, either. Told you I had to do something first. I slipped them off in the Ladies."

His voice fell a notch "So, if I were to run my hand up your leg, beneath your skirt..." He stepped closer, backing her up until her shoulders touched the wall.

"You'd find my thigh a little wet."

He dropped to his knees. "And if I ran my tongue along your wet thigh?" He pushed her skirt up, trailed his fingers up her leg.

"You'd find the pot of gold at the end of the rainbow."

He touched her slick folds. "Liquid gold," he murmured before burying his face between her legs. It took less than a minute and Lexi was convulsing around his tongue. Streams of juice poured from her, coating Adam's mouth.

He waited for the last tremor to pass, and then stood, stripping his pants down as he did. In one fluid movement, he grabbed her hips and lifted her. At the same time, she pushed back against the wall and jumped, wrapping her legs around his waist and her arms around his shoulders. He was embedded in her tingling body before she'd straightened her back.

"Lexi. God, that's good."

He filled her, stretched her and took her to paradise again with a few hard thrusts. Then he joined her there. He let go and jettisoned his release deep inside of her. The freedom and ease with which he did it pushed her and she rode him harder, enjoyed the way her second orgasm stretched out to encompass his.

When he finally pulled out, set her down and collapsed against her, she relished the drops of his come trickling down her thigh.

"The auto start's going to kick on in about two minutes," she said. "The doors are gonna roll open and everyone's gonna know what we've done." She gave a soft laugh. "The evidence is dribbling down my leg."

For the second time in five minutes, he got down on his knees. "Can't have that," he told her. "The only one who gets to find out about this particular pot of gold is me." He proceeded to lick her clean. He started on her left shin and worked his way up, lapping at the sticky mess. He repeated the procedure on the other leg, and then started on her folds.

"Christ, Adam." That had to be the sexiest thing he'd ever done. She gasped as he tried to remove every last trace of evidence. "It's not working." His attempts were counterproductive. Every lick of his tongue made her hotter, wetter, and she was soon climaxing for a third time as his mouth closed over her clit and sucked.

Adam rose, wiped his mouth clean and kissed her briefly. Then he did up his pants while she buttoned her top with shaky hands. Her skirt dropped back into place as the lift doors slid open.

"I love you, Adam Riley," she told him as another couple stepped inside.

"I love you too, Lexi Tanner," he answered.

"Riley," she corrected.

"I love you too, Lexi Riley," he said and smiled the traffic stopper.

About the Author

To learn more about Jess Dee, please visit www.jessdee.com.

Send an email to jess@jessdee.com or visit her at MySpace at www.myspace.com/writerjessdee.

He found her handcuffed to his bed. Can they unchain her memories in time to save her life?

Lost But Not Forgotten
© 2007 Mackenzie McKade

When pharmaceutical researcher Alexis Knight returns home from the Amazon jungle in a quest to reclaim the year of her life lost to amnesia, she discovers a host of changes have taken place in her absence. Not only has the shy, geeky boy she knew years ago transformed into a virile, confident hunk, he's bought her family home and is in the process of turning her late mother's bedroom into a den of iniquity.

When Jake O'Malley finds spitfire Allie handcuffed to his bed, accused of breaking and entering, his first thought is that his dreams have been served up to him on a platter. Then he realizes she's not acting when she says she doesn't remember the past year, nor her own mother's death.

As Jake eases Allie past her grief, her journey to reclaim her memories entwines with an exploration into the world of BDSM. Just as their psychological duel to dominate heats up, they make another, more chilling discovery.

There's a reason Allie lost her memory—someone wants her dead.

Available now in ebook and print from Samhain Publishing.

Enjoy the following excerpt from Lost But Not Forgotten:

Crap. Allie hightailed it toward her bedroom, shutting the door just before Jake burst from the bathroom.

The pounding on her bedroom door startled her, but she didn't move.

"You little witch. Open this door." Jake didn't sound too happy.

"Serves you right," she shouted at the closed door. The pipes in the house had always been a little finicky. She had learned that much as a child. Too many times, she had begun to bathe just as her mother started the dishes. The result was hot or cold water—never anything in between.

Truth was she could use a cold shower about now. It had taken all her strength not to accept what Jake offered, a night in his arms. Even now, her body burned with need.

Allie's heart raced as she leaned against the locked door. >From the other side, Jake shook it so that she felt the tremor clear to her bones.

"Allie, let me in," he growled.

"Beat all you want. You're not getting in here." Vibrations from his pounding continued to shake the door. Abruptly, they stopped. Allie harrumphed. "Giving up so soon?" A chuckle of satisfaction rose and died as quickly.

She shouldn't have taken her temper out on Jake. Everything that had happened recently was overwhelming. She was in trouble—big trouble.

Jake had been good to her mother—good to her. He didn't have to let her stay here. Truth was this wasn't her house. But that hadn't stopped her from making an appointment to meet with her mother's lawyer tomorrow.

The click of the lock sent her into action. "Oh, shit!" Allie flung herself against the door, but it was too late. Jake rushed through still only wearing the towel low around his hips. The inertia sent her backward and she fell on her ass. Pain radiated up her spine.

"Sonofabitch!" *That hurts.*

Before she could rise on her own, Jake yanked her to her feet, firmly against his solid chest. The lines on his face were hardened, but his eyes were not.

Damn man was enjoying himself. Her anger flared anew, racing like a wildfire across her cheeks.

He gave her a little shake. "I ought to jerk you across my lap and beat your ass."

She glared at him. "You wouldn't dare."

Jake released her, except for the iron grip he had on her right arm. "The hell you say." He began to drag her toward the bed.

Planting her heels into the worn carpet, she balled her freed fist and swung.

With lightning speed, he caught the punch and slammed her back against the wall. The air in her lungs gushed out on impact. She recovered quickly, countering with a raised knee to his groin that missed its mark. Just in time, he swung away only returning to pin her flat against the wall with his unyielding body.

Trapped. She couldn't move—couldn't breathe, except for the spicy, masculine scent that assailed her.

Damn. He was good. He knew her way too well, anticipating every defensive move she made.

"Release me or I'll—"

In a surprise response, he stole her threat away with a

punishing kiss.

There was no gentleness in his touch. Teeth meshed with teeth. His invasion was demanding, forceful, as his tongue pushed past her tight lips. Fast and skillfully, he tasted every inch of her mouth.

Her struggles for release were futile. He was bigger—stronger—and his body covered hers like a shield.

This definitely wasn't the boy she knew.

Allie whimpered, caught between anger and the slow burn he stirred inside her as he ground his hips to hers. His arousal pressed tight against her belly. His masterful kiss plucked the strings of her desire, pulling her deeper and deeper under his control.

But he wouldn't win, she swore to herself, even when his warm hand slid between the folds of her silky robe. Yet when his fingertips worked past her camisole to cup her breast, she silently screamed, *No! You won't win—*

Her breath caught as he squeezed her nipple.

Sweet pain splintered through her breast as he increased the pressure. The radiating sensation filtered through her globe, heading down south to tighten low in her belly.

Anger and need collided, releasing a fresh wave of desire between her thighs.

It had been forever since she'd made love, felt her body satisfied.

The truth was she needed to be held. With everything that had happened, Allie needed a strong man's arms around her more than anything.

Before Allie could change her mind, she wadded her hands in the towel around his waist and pulled. The deep rumble in his throat only heated her blood more. Her fingertips weaved through his light dusting of chest hair. Within seconds, he had her devoid of her robe, camisole, and panties, her heavy breasts against his moist chest.

For a moment, he didn't speak and only stared at her breasts. The desire in his eyes stoked the fire inside her.

Again, he captured her lips in a fiery kiss, hungry and fierce. His smoothed his palms slowly up the outside of her thighs, then moved inward. She inched her legs apart, waiting breathlessly as he skimmed closer to her pussy.

A deep growl vibrated next to her neck sending a shiver through her.

His fingers played across her skin. Every place he touched sparked with life.

His gaze was hot—sultry.

She released a squeal as he pushed her back against the cool, stucco wall and lifted her off her feet.

"Wrap your legs around my waist." His voice was a dark seduction, so demanding.

She locked her ankles behind his waist, pressing his erection hard against her wet folds. Before she could weave her arms around his neck, he captured both wrists in one large hand and held them high above her head. He looped his other arm beneath her ass. His body did the rest to keep her suspended.

"Jake—"

She tried to suck in a much-needed breath, but he took that moment to shift his hips and drive his cock deep inside her.

"*Ahhh...*" she groaned. Jake was so large it took a moment for her body to soften and receive him. When he moved deeper, filling her completely, all thought, not to mention argument, fled from her mind. Her only coherent reflection was how wonderful he felt buried inside her. Then he began to thrust, not gently, but hard and fast.

Oh God. It was heavenly.

Allie had never had a man fit her so perfectly—one who made her pussy hum as he did, moving in and out of her body. Every muscle tightened with delight, every nerve ending came alive.

Stinging rays shot up her chamber. "Jake!" she screamed, writhing against him. Hands pinned above her head, she jerked for release, but it was useless.

He slammed into her body with a force she felt at the back of her womb. Her orgasm moved closer and closer. She needed what lingered just out of reach, driving her insane, as her breasts rasped against his chest.

"Come for me," he rumbled.

GREAT
CHEAP
FUN

Discover eBooks!

THE FASTEST WAY TO GET THE HOTTEST NAMES

Get your favorite authors on your favorite reader, long before they're
out in print! Ebooks from Samhain go wherever you go, and work with
whatever you carry—Palm, PDF, Mobi, and more.

Samhain
Publishing Ltd

WWW.SAMHAINPUBLISHING.COM

Printed in the United States
142985LV00003B/20/P

9 781599 988139